FAÇADE

PEPPER BASHAM

Facade

Copyright © 2018 by Pepper D Basham

Published by

Woven Words

9 Cedar Trail, Asheville, NC

All rights reserved.

No part of this publication may be reproduced in any form, stored in a retrieval system, posted on any website, or transmitted in any form by any means—digital, electronic, scanning, photocopy, recording, or otherwise—without prior written permission from the publisher, except for brief quotations in printed reviews and articles.

This book is a work of fiction. Names, characters, places and incidents either are the product of the author's imagination or are used fictitiously, and any resemblance to actual persons, living or dead, business establishments, events, or locales is entirely coincidental.

Cover image ©2018 by Roseanna White Designs & Pepper D Basham

Cover art photos ©iStockphoto.com and Pixabay used by permission.

Published in the United States of America by Pepper Basham

www.pepperdbasham.com

To the men and women who gave or risked their lives to free others

CHAPTER 1

Yet another grand display of extravagance and the idiosyncrasies of the social dance.

Olivia Rakes sat in the corner of the lavish ballroom of her parents' London townhouse, watching the couples on the dance floor move in perfect synchrony as if part of one of the new moving picture shows. She preferred her hidden spot, shadowed by the recess in the ornate wall, just enough so her father could note her presence but not so apparent that unmarried men presented themselves to ask ridiculous questions like, "May I have this dance?"

She despised dancing, and when the spinning was paired with the busy, wine-colored wallpaper of the opulent room, Livy couldn't understand how more people didn't become dizzy.

Perhaps her myriad unwelcome partners skewed her interest, along with the added pressure of her mother's matrimonial exploits to salvage her woefully unattached eldest daughter's prospects. Unlike her younger sister, Livy had never found a suitable partner for dancing, conversation, or the vague and somewhat daunting task of marriage. Though not for her mother's grand and glorious attempts, leading to a failed engagement, one or two disappointed would-be suitors, and a dozen disastrous dinner parties.

Thankfully, her younger sister fulfilled their mother's lifelong dream with an early marriage and now a burgeoning middle that held her first child. If Charlie married some rich countess then their mother's dreams would be complete, leaving Livy to enjoy an introverted, book-wealthy, and academic future of joyous spinsterhood.

She glanced about the Victorian-styled room again and stifled the slightest cringe. A future in a simple cottage with as many windows as bookshelves…and no ballrooms.

Music started anew and couples once again moved to the center of the room. Livy pressed farther into her nook, pulling her latest Miss Marple mystery from her near-empty bag. What else did one need? A pen, pencil, notepad, and an Agatha Christie novel all fit within the folds of her largest reticule, and a novel provided a perfect distraction from the party.

Her mother used the excuse of a new war to resurrect the old style and flamboyance of a benefit ball, but, of course, any excuse for extravagance provided fuel enough. At least this parade of glitz and glamour held some purpose—a fundraiser for the men at war. Livy grimaced. The thought of her brother zooming through the skies of France left her stomach in a spiraling crunch.

Dear Charlie. The only person in the whole world who appreciated her particular brand of eccentricity. How she missed him.

She kept abreast of war news for his sake, to follow whatever exploits he was at liberty to share in his letters, and in the desperate hope she'd never hear his name read among the dead or missing. Surely, God knew her brother would prove much more useful alive than injured behind enemy lines or buried unknown in German-occupied France.

A sudden shadow fell over her from the next room, and she stifled a groan.

"Miss Rakes?"

With a muted sigh, she closed her book and returned it to her reticule. Before her stood a smiling older gentleman, his pale eyes familiar in some distant sort of way. The pieces would click together soon enough. She never forgot a face. "Yes?"

"I do not know if you remember me. I have been in America for a few years now and have only recently returned."

She scratched the back of her mind to find him, clarity emerging through the other faces in her memory. Ah yes, one of her father's contemporaries. "Captain Dawson."

His smile relaxed with friendly relief. "Yes, it's been..."

"At least three years?"

He laughed in the cheerful way she remembered so well that the sound inspired her own smile. "Much too long to be away from home, if you ask me."

"It depends on the home, I should think." She studied him and took his outstretched hand, remembering the scratch of his fingers and palms worn from his time on the seas. "And I've known you my whole life, sir. How could I not remember you?"

"Your sister still has no recollection of either Christopher or I."

Christopher! Oh, she remembered *him*. An arrogant boy who was forever trying to best her in every competition known to man. Tennis, fox hunting, chess, wits... She grinned at the recollection of the fiery-tempered, gangly youth. Unnervingly memorable. He'd never bested her at wits, though he had made admirable attempts to soften her rather abrupt comments in social situations.

And he'd been an excellent partner at cards, with a solid chivalrous streak.

She'd always appreciated his chivalry. His gallant and thoughtful behavior softened the sharp edges of him in her reminiscence, especially the memory of his impolite disappearance from her life. She pinched her lips into a tight line. He didn't deserve a smile, not even in memory. Cruel man. What sort of friend disappears without a logical explanation—or an explanation at all, as a matter of fact.

"What brings you home, Captain?"

"War, I'm afraid." He grumbled the response, his good-natured surliness one of the reasons Livy had liked him from the start. "My work as a consultant with the American ambassador is better served here in more intricate ways."

His eyes sparkled with a glint she knew all too well, and she wrenched her rebel curiosity under control. *Not again!* Military men looking for scapegoats in their war against technology, force, and brutality. Captain Dawson's allure lost a little of its sheen. Since 1940 officials had been recruiting some of the smartest women Livy knew, and not even a year after their previous attempt, they'd found her again, this time using a family friend.

Well, they were persistent, she'd give them that.

The American influence in his speech came through mostly in his vowels, hinting at time spent in the northern parts of the United States rather than the southern.

"Intricacies can become entangling and I'm not fond of feeling entangled, Captain. Are you?"

"Not at all. Nor am I fond of war, my dear." He laughed and offered her a hand. "But I am fond of dancing and would greatly enjoy the opportunity to become reacquainted with you."

Livy shot her father a knowing glare, but he, in perfect fatherly form, only raised his glass in a mock toast celebrating his accomplishment of stealing her from her hiding spot. With an eye roll for his benefit, she placed her hand in the captain's and moved to the floor.

Women wore elegant gowns of the latest fashions, their bodies molded into hourglasses shaped by the miraculous contortion of undergarments. Red lips and nails boasted the American inspiration of the day while sculpted hair curled into various-sized rolls away from their faces. Quite unnatural, to Livy's mind, but most people didn't care for what was going on in Livy's mind unless they wanted her for translations, unwanted matrimony, or espionage.

She highly doubted Captain Dawson desired a conversation regarding the first two of the three options.

Livy's rather plain burgundy gown fit as well as the rest of her. Understated. An observer. Just as she preferred. The rollicking pace of big band music energized the room with brass, piano, and the deep strums of the bass. The players were the best her father's money could afford and did not disappoint. Ah, the consolation of being in such tight quarters with the local social monarchy—excellent music.

"Your father tells me you are working in linguistics at University College."

Sigh. Small talk. The language she liked least of all. It either meant nothing or proved a preamble to something people refused to say plainly. "Yes, I am an assistant to a professor there."

"And you were previously educated at French *Lycee*, yes?"

Why were all of them so predictable? "Yes."

"Do you still have your clever little gift? The one of observation?"

Did all recruitment officers begin their conversations the same way? Livy sliced through the slosh with a direct answer. "Captain, though your accent has been influenced by your recent life in northern America, I can tell that you've since traveled abroad to India. Your arrival from that country has been within the week and must have left you without valet or wife due to the nature of your overgrown moustache and sideburns as well as the wrinkles in your collar." She narrowed her eyes at his shock and examined him some more. "Your sudden intake of breath at the mention of your wife may point to an unhappy dissolution but I certainly hope not. Divorces are rather nasty affairs, and Mrs. Dawson always appeared to be quite charming. You're not-so-subtle execution of this dance and subsequent interview informs me that you are seeking agents for some undercover or cypher work, and I can only guess that you are desperate by contacting me."

He sputtered, stumbled through a few of the dance steps, and then blinked at her. "I...you...your father wasn't exaggerating."

"Knowing my father, I'm certain he was, but I am curious about your wife."

"We had an argument, and she's visiting her mother in Yorkshire."

Livy's lips softened into a smile. "No divorce then?"

He blinked again, his generous moustache shivering from exhalation. "I certainly hope not. Especially over hyacinths."

Livy's full laugh broke forth—an underused expression for her part. "Those must have been some rather impressive hyacinths."

"*Were* impressive, I'm afraid."

She cringed, and another laugh bubbled out unbidden. "I see the rash separation choice then, Captain. Better a short visit to her mother than a forever visit elsewhere, yes?"

"Exactly. And my valet took ill on our return trip from India."

"I am sorry, on both counts."

His grin spread, and he chuckled. "You *are* impressive. And fluent in several languages, I understand."

Oh, why couldn't he let her have a successful conversation without the addition of an agenda to combat.

"Three, other than English, of course." She smiled to keep up appearances, but since she'd failed quite swimmingly thus far, the effort proved rather pointless. "French, German, and Italian, with some minor studies in Latin and Greek."

"That is excellent! Did you know that Christopher is fluent in German and French as well?" The man's blatant intentions turned with the gesture of his hand to someone in the crowd. Livy pinched her eyes closed and released a longsuffering sigh. *Dreaded reinforcements.*

Across the room walked a man wholly familiar yet surprisingly unfamiliar. His blond locks had muted into a dusty color with streaks of the former slicked back into a fashionable style away from his face. Once-pale eyes shone a darker blue, so alarming her pulse ricocheted into a responsive jitter. The years had treated him kindly. Very kindly. Traitors, those years!

His expression revealed nothing, except perhaps a slight annoyance directed at her. Ah, he looked even more familiar. She remembered that disapproving grimace all too well, especially at her engagement party. She'd never seen him so out of sorts in their entire friendship—and she was certain her distinct personality gave him plenty of opportunities to be out of sorts.

Then he'd disappeared.

Suddenly, he looked decidedly less handsome.

"Livy."

She wasn't certain why she'd expected formality, but his utter lack of it stole any clever response she'd concocted at his approach. A baritone rumble of consonants and vowels emerged, evoking a pleasant trill of tingles up her neck. She refused to consider what those tingles meant and instead put them into motion, tilting her chin up to focus on his chiseled face.

"Would you mind taking my place in the dance, son? I feel the need to rest my feet."

Christopher's surprise flickered but recovered with a rather fascinating smile. "Of course."

A plastic smile, if she remembered anything. The kind that spoke just the opposite of his desire. Yes, she remembered lots of things, and with such clarity her face warmed at her old friend's closeness.

"I think the two of you have much to discuss."

Livy stifled a groan and stiffened her body as Christopher's hand slid to her waist. Her words lodged in her throat on an intake of air. Why did his touch feel much different than his father's? No wonder these men were a part of the elite force on espionage! They used distraction as a clear tool to get what they wanted.

A rush of lightning fire flew from her chest into her cheeks. Well, she wouldn't be so easily persuaded, handsome childhood friend or not. *Oh, the tangled web we weave....*

～

His father would not get away with this unscathed. Christopher grimaced into the face of his former playmate, her large, gray eyes as changeful as ever. Unnerving. Challenging. Well, at least this competition he won in height. Her style and makeup, or lack thereof, proved she'd kept the same personality she'd possessed three years earlier. Impress with wits, not appearance, though even her natural beauty, when paired with her innate rebellion, held a certain charm.

Charm enough to steal a man's heart...then break it.

No, she was *not* a good choice for their operation. Not at all.

"It's been a long time," he muttered, searching for conversation to fill the awkward reintroduction and subsequent silence.

"Yes."

Her smirk grounded him. "And you've pursued more languages so you can correct the world at large, I suspect."

Those gray eyes darkened to a strange pale green. Ah, he still knew how to hit his mark. The knowledge produced an unwelcome curl of warmth in his chest that hollowed into loss. She'd chosen someone else. Not him.

"Improving the world one person at a time, Mr. Dawson, though I feel I owe you an apology for failing where you're concerned."

His grin slid crooked and three years shrunk to seconds. "No, you haven't changed much at all."

"And you have? An inch or two of added height doesn't get at the core." Her gaze roamed his face, brow furrowed in such scrutiny he almost squirmed. "Sun. Hmm... You've been working outdoors. You didn't accompany your father to India, so you were either left in America or here?" She squinted. "Up to no good, I'd wager?"

"I would call you a busybody if I didn't know your secret power." He leaned closer. "A power my father believes is wasted on the young minds at University College."

One dark brow, the same shade as her pinned hair, edged north. "My dear Mr. Dawson, why don't you come out and quite plainly say what you mean? This shilly shallying around wastes blessed time and efficiency."

A sudden bubble of frustration set him into motion. The world quaked from a war devastating Europe, men were dying by the second, and she had the gall to accuse him of wasting time? He'd spent the last four months scouring the country in search of people with the skill set and the willingness to infiltrate German-occupied France. He'd lost friends and colleagues. And now this *childhood* friend whose family lived off old money and attempted to tamp the flame of war with benefit balls charged him with being inefficient?

Without thinking, he took her arm and drew her from the dance floor. He'd installed himself as the one who would set Livy Rakes in place when he was twelve and she ten, and it appeared he still held the occupation years later.

He ignored her glare beating into his profile and zigzagged beyond the elaborate furnishings into the hallway. But for decoration, the house hadn't changed in twelve years since he'd first stepped into it as an eleven-year-old boy. With Livy whispering protests behind him, no time could have passed at all.

He opened a coat closet and pulled her inside.

"You want directness, Miss Rakes?" He flipped the switch on the wall, and a dim light flooded the small room, hollowing her large eyes even further.

Her eyes had always been his downfall—the mirror into the soul she fisted behind books and isolation. She stood close enough that the faintest hint of rosewater permeated the coat smell around him, enticing another deep breath. He'd fallen in love with the scent of roses because of her.

"I see three years have made little difference in your personality, Mr. Dawson." Oh, three years made an enormous difference. Training, secrets, a world swarmed with uncertainty, and a heart still nursing the pangs of her engagement to another man. All the wounds he'd smothered beneath denial wrenched awake as if not one day had passed. For his own sake, he had to prove that Olivia Rakes was not spy material.

THE CLOSET?

Livy fought the coats pushing her closer to Christopher's body. They'd hidden in this closet countless times as children, but the space seemed much larger then, with room to breathe and maneuver without knocking into one another. The aroma of vanilla mixed with sweet butter swarmed around her. Oakmoss. The closet shrunk a little more and her throat grew curiously dry.

He'd started wearing it a year before he left, a soft and warm scent like his presence had always been. A friendship she hadn't missed until he'd disappeared. She hadn't understood how their relationship mattered to such a degree that his absence left a hole no amount of studying and reading could fill. A hole that, at the moment, loomed larger than ever, and filled her with unanswered questions. How could he have gone? Why did he leave? Friends didn't treat each other with such flagrant disregard...if she knew anything about friendship at all.

"I've done my research on you, Livy." He edged a little closer, his presence almost mesmerizing in the dim lights. "You appreciate research, don't you?"

She would not let him affect her sensibilities no matter how much his oakmoss aftershave lingered in the air like a drug or how his gaze searched hers with a gentleness that somehow sought to rekindle the friendship he'd tossed aside.

"It solely depends on the research. At present my information leads me to wonder at your purpose in drawing me into a closet. Is it a customary practice of yours to bring women into closets, or has your reputation fallen since you were twenty? Perhaps it's a diversion you learned in the States?" His glare somehow made hiding in the closet worthwhile. "I should think with your family's longstanding military history, both in this country and America, you'd be more cautious."

He gave her a beautifully delivered scowl. "We've been friends a long time." The statement made its mark, and her heart still responded to the claim as if he'd never left. An ache reopened in her chest.

He nudged closer, his eyes dancing with a determined flame. "And as your friend, I have been tasked with pointing out your potential and possible purpose."

Friend? Indeed! She scoffed. "My purpose?"

"You work very hard in your position as assistant to linguistics expert Professor Archibald Murphy, to which you receive the bulk of the work and he receives the bulk of the praise."

The admission stung but she captured a rebuttal. "Mark my words, within five years we'll see a female appointment to a professorship. We are proving our abilities in academia. America isn't the only forward-thinking country on the globe."

"Then why don't you prove your skillset in the field? We're at war and the cost has been much greater than anyone anticipated." Christopher ran a hand through his rich swath of intermingled golden hair. "You can't pretend you've not been approached before. I know of two instances, Livy."

A sweet internal tremor accompanied each time he said her name. She frowned at its unwelcome violation to her cool-headedness, but her heart welcomed to the sensation. She'd missed him. There was something incredibly attractive about a man who engaged in such excellent arguments. Yes, she'd missed this, their tête-a-têtes. She almost smiled. There were too few men up to the task of a good verbal sparring.

"The Government Code and Cypher School sought you to join their elite team of code breakers at Bletchley but you refused."

"Regretfully declined would be a better way to word it. Besides, I am not well-suited to the mathematical component of that task. Languages? Linguistics? Observation? Yes. But numbers, no."

"And you also refused a request from the Special Operations Executive."

"I have no interest in using my womanly wiles to ascertain how prepared male spies are for the temptations of the field. As I'm certain you know, with your extended knowledge of me." She waved a hand toward herself. "My mother's already branded me a spinster, which is in part due to my charming personality." She swallowed a laugh at his glare of utter doubt. "The other part I blame wholly on the weak constitution of most men to appreciate a confident woman and their inability to engage in fidelity. When the cat's away...you understand."

"You have a very low opinion of most men."

"The way of the world would prove me right, don't you think? Let us not forget, my darling fiancé lasted only one month before his heart was swayed by another."

Christopher's expression took a turn she couldn't decipher but somehow beckoned her nearer. "And he broke you heart?"

She laughed. "Goodness, no. The only man in my life who broke my heart was you."

A shot of air escaped his open mouth. "Me?"

Her gaze lifted to his, a river of uncertainty stealing the fire of her accusations. Could he truly be surprised by her declaration? "How... how could you just leave? After all our years together? Nothing but a card at Christmas and birthdays? Wasn't our friendship worth more than that? Clearly I underestimated the mutual attachment."

He stared at her, tension fading from his face by slow degrees. Something akin to regret dawned in those cerulean eyes. "I...I shouldn't have left that way. It was irresponsible and unkind."

"Indeed." She stepped away from him. "A little late for clarity, isn't it, Christopher? Three years late."

"You really had no idea?" He groaned and ran a hand through his hair. "You wouldn't understand."

"Yet you think me clever enough to engage in espionage?"

"It's different, Livy. Worlds different. But I was wrong. I reacted blindly from my anger and disappoint—"

"*Your* disappointment?" She closed in, the sting of pain pushing past her logic. "We'd been friends..." She shrugged, recalling their consistent arguments and intense discussions over books they'd read and philosophies they didn't share. "Or at least friendly antagonists who'd developed a relationship over habitual time and conversations. You were a...a fixture."

An unfriendly laugh accompanied a shake of his head. "A fixture? Yes, that would be a clear definition. How engaging you make friendship sound, my dear Livy."

"So, you would call it friendship then, would you?" She shot him a glare. "Well, your employment of friendship leaves as much to be desired as my definition."

He growled and took her by the arm. "As much as I'd like to clear the air, or at the very least shake some sense into you, I can't have the discussion about my reasons for leaving right now. We haven't time." He cleared his throat and leveled her with those intense eyes of his. "Why not take your excellent confidence and apply it. You completed the training for the SOE then left. Why?"

Heat slid from her body. Her first assignment had dissolved into a circumstance that led to her partner's capture and death. The entire situation had been a setup, in broad daylight, just over the border in northern France. A simple gathering of information for her first trial turned into the murder of her partner, who had been more experienced and sacrificed herself so Livy could escape. The scenario replayed among the agents, tales of sacrifice for the lives of others, but the feelings of failure overran any glory in the work. Livy would not fail again, especially at the expense of another life.

"I haven't the stomach for it."

"The stomach for it?" He released his hold on her and folded his arms across his chest, resembling a disgruntled school teacher. "Time may have done many things to you, but it hasn't softened your determined character. Our offices wouldn't continue to seek you out if you didn't possess valuable skills to the cause. My father believes your gift of observation and keen senses will help protect men like your brother."

At the mention of Charlie, Livy's argument stilled on her tongue. Before Bletchley and the SOE, Charlie had been safely home, or at the very least in aviator training, but now he piloted somewhere over France. A daring and charismatic occupation for a daring and charismatic man.

She blamed Christopher Dawson for the fact her eyes stung in a most annoying way. "Then I shall pray, raise money for the cause, and continue my weekly volunteering at the local war hospital."

He stepped toward her, her gaze intense, alive. "You are not a coward, Livy. You never have been."

Oakmoss and the scent of failure squeezed around her. She reached for the door knob. "Mr. Dawson, I'm most flattered by the government's faith in me." Her throat tightened around the words, almost as if her body refused to acquiesce to the cowardice in her statement. "And I sincerely hope you find the people you need to end this war, but I am not one of them."

CHAPTER 2

This war had taken a far bloodier turn than anyone anticipated, and the last thing Christopher needed on his mind was another regret. But the look on Livy's face as they'd argued in the closet at the benefit burned through his conscience with the sting of a Luger PO8 bullet. He rubbed his shoulder at the tangible memory of a close call, the wound not too far from the one aching around his heart.

His pace down the sidewalk doubled along with his breaths on his march to his parents' townhouse. He needed a long evening alone in his room to recover from the events of the day. A light mist coated the evening air and curled his smooth hair into an unruly mop. No matter. There were much more sobering things to consider. He took off his hat and beat it against his leg. Like the painful news of another downed agent—a woman, this time.

Anna Graves had been her real name, but only a few people on the team knew Clarissa Dubois by the moniker. He'd been one. German airmen had shot down her plane over France during the SOE's most recent search-and-rescue mission for lost boys held behind enemy lines.

He rubbed at the tension in his forehead as the streetlamps of home shone into view.

It was a good thing Livy refused his request. The very thought of her in such danger twisted his insides to knots.

He sighed and slowed his pace. He'd been a fool three years ago—a wounded fool. Jealous, angry, hurt, and had responded accordingly without a thought of how his actions might impact her. After all, she'd pushed him out of her life months before her engagement, engrossed in her studies and her mother's matchmaking mayhem.

He replayed her look of sheer confusion and hurt from the week before when they'd holed up in the closet during the benefit. Yes, they had been friends, and he'd hoped they'd become much more. He fisted his hands and walked toward the townhouse, replaying their conversation as he bypassed a couple and their oversized brolly on the sidewalk. And she'd cast him off as an unimportant *fixture,* hadn't she?

Why was he even pondering Livy Rakes and her intentions? A war was on and he would leave in two weeks to train new recruits. He didn't need her or her changeling eyes fogging his clarity. Yet, dislodging her from his musings proved as difficult now as it had been three years ago.

The ache in his chest intensified to such a degree that after climbing the steps to the townhouse door he almost passed Walken, their stodgy butler, without a greeting.

"Pardon me, Walken. I'm preoccupied this evening."

"Not at all, sir." Walken assisted Christopher with his jacket. "Dinner is to be served at half past seven, sir."

"Thank you." Christopher made for the stairs to bypass either of his parents, so he could enjoy a few quiet moments alone to process the news about Anna Graves, but his father's keen hearing gave him away.

"Christopher? Is that you?"

Christopher pinched his eyes closed and released a long stream of air through his nose before turning to face his father. "I have a few papers to sort through before dinner but then we can talk."

"Very good. Very good." The words grumbled out from his father's mouth without any bite. "I wanted to prepare you that we have a guest joining us for dinner tonight."

Christopher curbed his shoulders from showing his disappointment and offered a nod. "Another colleague from work? Or one of Mother's friends?"

Christopher continued his climb up the stairs to the office he shared with his father for their mutual occupation, his father following a few steps behind. "Actually, a friend of yours."

"A friend of mine?"

The glimmer in his father's eyes shot a prelude of warning. Christopher began unbuttoning his suit jacket and sighed. "Father…"

"We can't just give up on her, son."

"Her?" He slipped out of his jacket and sifted through all the possibilities of their shared acquaintance with only one floating to the top. "You didn't."

"She's more than qualified."

"She said no."

His father shrugged one of his hefty shoulders. "Perhaps we'll changed her mind."

Christopher paused at the threshold of the office doorway and studied his father through narrowed eyes. "What did you promise her?"

"Your lack of faith wounds me." His father's palm went to his chest in mock pain. "Besides, I think she has softened a little since the benefit, and we offer a puzzle her quick mind hasn't worked out yet. So, I used it as leverage."

Christopher groaned and hung his head as he walked toward his desk. "And what puzzle could that possibly be?"

"You."

Christopher took a full turn to face his father. "Me?" He laughed and rounded the desk. "I believe your skills of deduction have lost their clarity, Father."

"As you've said many times in the past, Livy Rakes doesn't like unsolved mysteries, and you pose a challenge for her."

Christopher slacked into the desk chair, wishing his father's words didn't hold a nugget of hope that he fought to ignore. "I'm more of an annoyance than a curiosity, Father. She's made her decision regarding me quite clear."

His father raised a brow and a corner of his grin. "I know you still care about her."

Christopher spared his father a glare before shuffling through papers he didn't see, ignoring the inkling of truth the older man's declaration inspired. An unreachable itch he'd attempted to ignore for three years. But he'd played the fool before, and she'd pushed him away as a...fixture? The idea ground his determination even deeper. No, he would not seek out Livy again. No matter what optimism his father touted.

"And, I remember the two of you together, nigh inseparable for years." His father gaze failed to waver. "I wager, she cares about you much more than she even understands."

The weight Christopher had carried for years tripled in one breath along with another nudge of hope he thought he'd eradicated with enough time and distance. Their time together at the benefit proved Livy Rakes still held court over his heart, and he remained a fool. He'd gone to sleep with her wounded expression and her rosewater scent tempting delirium every night since their closet rendezvous. *Weak-willed idiot of a man! What will it take for you to learn your lesson?*

But why did his affections cease to turn in her direction? Why couldn't he squeeze her out of his life for good? She'd been able to do so, hadn't she? "Father, there is a war going on. I really don't have time to dabble in your theories about my heart or Livy Rakes's."

Silence pulled Christopher's attention across the room to where his father stood. The older man's face tightened into a look his former seamen must have cowered beneath. It stilled every muscle in Christopher's body. "Yes indeed, war is here...and a further reminder that time and people are not commodities to be taken lightly."

Christopher hesitated in that knowing look, the thought searing his conscience with a truth he reproached with a list of memories. He couldn't...he *wouldn't*...fall again. "You realize pursuing her when she's made up her mind about a matter is going to push her away."

His father released the tautness in his stance and rocked back on his heels. "Sometimes pursuing a woman is exactly what a woman wants a man to do. To show her that she's worth the cost, the sacrifice, the risk." His steely gaze sent all sorts of obvious messages. "I may be old and not as savvy in the ways of romance as I once was, but I don't believe Olivia Rakes is as certain of herself or her heart as you believe. Confidence in a profession does not automatically carryover to other, more intimate, areas of life."

Christopher returned his attention to his papers. "She makes her mind up rather decidedly, Father."

The former captain backed toward the office door. "Her mind is one thing. Her heart is another. I'm not certain the two are in agreement." He patted the doorframe as if he hadn't just set up the most uncomfortable evening of the year. "I can't think of one woman who doesn't appreciate a solid pursuit from a man she has feelings for."

"Oh, she most certainly has feelings for me. None of them are good."

"And why is that, I wonder? For a man of your profession, I'm surprised your curiosity hasn't encouraged you to uncover what truly happened three years ago."

Wounded pride? Broken heart?

His father crossed over the threshold of the room into the hallway, his soft-spoken words just audible enough to reach Christopher's ears. "Perhaps to be as keen as she is in observing facts and details, she really has no idea of the many facets of the heart…especially her own?"

"I won't encourage her to join." His voice paused his father's exit. "It's too dangerous."

His father tipped a grin over his shoulder as if whatever Christopher said proved some point or other.

He stared at his father's retreating form, pinching the papers in his hands until they crimped. With a long sigh, he lowered his hands to the desk and allowed his mind to sift through the memories from a perspective less tainted with hurt. Could she have been as clueless to her own carelessness with his feelings as his father thought? All those missed appointments? All those unanswered letters? Surely not! Weren't men known as the sex to overlook the details of the heart, not women?

But Livy wasn't like any other woman he knew.

And he wouldn't place her on the same lines as Anna Graves and so many other women. Having her discard him was one thing. Losing her altogether was another.

And that very sentiment proved him the fool all over again.

CHAPTER 3

Desperation never sounded pleasant in anyone's voice, especially a sea captain's.

Livy almost turned around three times before she completed the short walk from her townhouse down the quiet street to the Dawson's, but she'd given her word to Captain Dawson when he made his grand plea. She wouldn't back out of what was sure to be another façade of pleading for her to join the SEO, but she wouldn't cave to his request either.

She'd warned him that her decision was made, but still he'd asked and offered a little incentive she couldn't turn down. Then there was the irrepressible curiosity of Christopher Dawson's return into her life.

His image blurred into her focus at work in the most annoying ways. She'd even called one of the young students by *his* name! Luckily, the young woman's name was Christine, so none was the wiser, but Livy had never left in such befuddlement.

Now he was within reach of a face-to-face confrontation. She grinned, purpose infusing her steps. For good or ill, she'd get to the bottom of his disappearance and move on with her life. Even if his excuse proved painful, nothing was worse than the unknown or unresolved. It released her mind to myriad possibilities much worse than reality, in most cases.

The Dawson's townhouse was smaller and simpler than her parents', a peek at the slight social gap between the two families, but Mrs. Dawson, whom Livy was glad to see had returned home after the hyacinths debacle, took Livy into her arms as if no time or misunderstanding had passed at all. "I cannot tell you how happy I was to know you'd accepted Arthur's invitation, dear Livy. It's been too long."

The woman wore the past three years without a blemish. Even her hairstyle remained a simple halo of gold flaked with silver threads in a style Livy's mother wore five years ago. Mary Dawson was the kind of person one wanted greeting you after a long absence because she remained recognizable, dependable, and stable. For Livy, whose mother's emotions ebbed and flowed with uneasy uncertainty, a warm greeting from Mary Dawson brought a great sense of calm Livy rarely experienced with others. Always had. There were enough distractions of mind in returning to a place one once knew without the aggravation of having to sort out who someone was.

"It's very good to see you again, Mrs. Dawson."

"Mary, please. We've moved beyond such formalities after all these years, don't you think?"

The manner of her son's behavior painted a little doubt on that statement. Livy flicked a gaze around the foyer in search of her traitor-friend, with only the reward of Captain Dawson's voice filtering in from the next room.

And the lingering essence of oakmoss.

He was here somewhere.

"I do apologize for the state of our home, but we've not kept up with the newest trends in decor." She waved toward the simple rosette wallpaper in the hallway. "It seems frivolous to spend money on redecorating when our boys on the frontline have so many needs."

A smile relaxed Livy's lips. She'd always appreciated Mary Dawson's sensibilities, her strength. "I'm fond of things remaining the same, Mrs. D— Mary. There's a comfort to consistency and predictability. It's quite sensible to my way of thinking."

Mrs. Dawson's laugh brought a warmth with it. "There you go

complimenting me, as you've done in the past, my dear Livy."

Livy stared at Mrs. Dawson, studying her for a hint of how she'd complimented the woman. She was one of those rare people who found sunshine in every situation. Usually Livy thought such behavior hinted towards duplicity, but not Mary Dawson's. She created a welcome calm Livy had grown to love and expect in the Dawson house. Though Livy loved her unpredictable socialite mother and aloof businessman of a father, Mary and Arthur Dawson introduced an anomaly of simple happiness.

Well, perhaps not so simple, especially in a world of war and brokenness and people vying for their own agendas. Somehow, these two kept their heads, hearts, and perspectives properly ordered. Livy smiled. No, not so simple.

"Though not as romantic as other options, I've always enjoyed being seen as a practical woman."

"Come now, Livy." Captain Dawson's voice boomed from the foyer as he entered the room. "Surely you want a little adventure. A woman in a man's field? A hearty academic? Those type of choices don't lend themselves to the timid of heart."

He took his wife's arm, and Livy followed them through the house, her attention on edge as they turned each corner. "Adventure is all well and good, Captain Dawson, but there's something to be said in staying right where God's put one at the moment." Her brow raised at his humored expression. "Not borrowing trouble."

He chuckled and led his wife to a place at the table. "Livy Rakes, you've spent your whole life borrowing trouble. Why change now?"

Her grin loosed. "In all honesty, I've always been perplexed by my uncanny ability to cause trouble. It's never my intention."

"It finds you, does it?" He winked as he drew out her chair for her.

"Or is thrust upon me?" Her gaze didn't leave his, needling her point at the agenda in his invitation.

His chuckle swelled into a good-natured laugh. "By some old codger in need of a miracle?" His expression softened, as if the thought of a miracle might be one of the most pleasant notions.

Because of the war? Her mind sifted through recent newspaper clippings she'd read, one after another detailing loss and destruction in

Belgium, France...anywhere the Germans stepped foot. Realization softened her slight annoyance at being asked to dinner as a ploy to join the agency. What Captain Dawson had seen must have impacted him in his desperation for assistance—any assistance—even hers.

His compassion pricked into her refusal, niggling her doubts to the forefront of her mind and heart. Could she help in this vast war? Even with her failure?

"Sorry to keep you all waiting." Christopher breezed into the room, drawing her attention from the captain. Her breath caught in her throat at his entrance, her cheeks pinking despite her attempts to remain neutral, even annoyed, toward her childhood friend.

She gripped her hands together in her lap to curb the slight irritation of the unexpected, especially when placed into a situation where the ground felt uneven beneath her. She liked making plans and following them through. This unexpected reunion brimmed with everything except blessed predictability.

Christopher grazed her with a look and a nod before taking his place across from her. The conversation remained civil and benign as the meal ensued, but despite her best attempts at keeping her thoughts under amiable indifference, her gaze pulled to him, studying, attempting to suss out why his absence mattered so much—and why his presence took up extensive space in her mind. Mrs. Dawson asked about Livy's job at the college, to which she gladly expounded with only a few dry comments from Captain Dawson regarding her tenacious personality.

Christopher remained unnervingly quiet. Watching her as much as she supposed she was watching him.

It all felt very much like walking on a thin layer of ice on a pond.

Or keeping to the tedious steps of an uncertain dance.

He didn't look like a scoundrel at all. For three years, she'd contorted his memory into one of an uncaring rake, a duplicitous rascal. Within tonight's setting, though he held his tongue, the gentle looks he sent to his mother and the smiles that passed between he and his father somehow reshaped her memories with a clearer brush.

Her old friend emerged—and with a renewed sting to her wound. Why had he left her?

"Oh Livy, we have such a surprise for you." Mary grinned and gestured toward the cook, who entered the room carrying a large dish as if she were delivering the crown jewels. "In your honor, Eliza has created her fabulous lemon tart. Do you remember it?"

Livy's attention shot to Christopher. Their gazes held, and the slightest corner of his mouth tilted. *Lemon tarts*. She hated lemons.

She offered Mrs. Dawson a smile—at least, what she hoped was a smile. "I recall it well." She'd gotten sick from it more than once, eating the dessert to appease the social expectation of accepting what was offered.

"The pork and vegetables were particularly filling tonight, Eliza. With such excellent seasoning, I think both Livy and I indulged. I'm not certain she has any room for your excellent dessert." Christopher's attention shifted from Eliza, flickered to Livy, and then rested on his mother. "Perhaps, you could send a slice or two home with her?"

Christopher Dawson was the most confusing sort of person. For a non-friend, he'd just been very friendly on her behalf, almost chivalrous considering her extreme aversion to lemons.

"Indeed." Her gaze hesitated in his before returning to the cook's. "And I'm certain my parents would be grateful recipients of your excellent skills as well, Eliza."

The woman beamed. "Then I shall make certain to add plenty to the tin, Miss Rakes."

"That's most kind of you, Eliza," Christopher added, his lips still crooked with mischief. "No one should miss your lemon tarts."

Livy stared at him. No wonder he was a spy. With no more than three sentences, he'd rescued her, smoothed over the possible slight with Eliza, *and* provided a coveted dessert for her father, who would sing its praises for weeks.

At dinner's end, Captain Dawson drew Livy into his office with another attempt to persuade her to join in the fight, but he didn't press her when she refused yet again, a little less certain than a week ago. With his usual grace, he escorted her from the room and caught Christopher coming toward them.

"You should see her home, son."

Christopher looked from his father to her, his expression waving into emotions she didn't comprehend but finally settling on resignation.

"I am quite capable of walking myself home," Livy interjected and began a direct line for the front door.

"But you don't *have* to." Christopher's voice came from close behind her. "And with the air raids, well, you *shouldn't* have to."

She glanced behind them through the doorway and lowered her voice. "I can take care of myself."

"You can." He searched her face with a sudden intensity she found mesmerizing and confusing. "But I will still walk you home."

Before she could refuse, he whisked to closet for his coat, and a strange mixture of emotions coursing through her vied for identification. Fear? Not exactly. Anticipation? She shook her head. But something hinged in her heart like an unfinished letter...and Christopher held the final lines.

Hope?

That seemed unlikely, didn't it?

He waved his brolly at her as he ushered her out the front door. "I see you're still not prepared for the rain, as usual."

She smiled up at the dingy, dark sky. "I rather like the rain. Consistent. Comforting. And a much better sound than the bombers flying overhead."

"And here I thought you wanted me to show my chivalrous side." He opened the brolly and stepped close enough for them to share, his arm brushing hers.

It took every ounce of willpower to bite back an unkind retort. Chivalrous? Yes, she'd once thought him so—in fact, less than an hour ago the thought crossed her mind—but pairing chivalry, even over a lemon tart rescue, and a disappearing friend left her unsettled all the more. Bothersome man!

They walked in silence as the light patter of rain tapped against their shelter. The scent of burned, damp wood interrupted the evening repose, an unwelcome reminder of a recent air raid's remains. Her brother likely flew somewhere within that giant dark sky tonight, his life on a constant precipice.

"I'm surprised you agreed to join us for dinner after your adamant refusal of Father's offer at the benefit."

She kept her gaze forward, but her thoughts buzzed with a fuzzy awareness of his nearness—a strange new distraction. They'd walked under umbrellas together for years. What had changed? "I wouldn't have come if he hadn't offered to donate to the linguistics department in my honor. I can certainly sit through an awkward dinner for the greater good of educational advancement." She stifled a grin but not well enough to cover it altogether. "It wasn't at all as awkward as I anticipated, though I do hope your father isn't too disappointed in a second refusal."

He turned slightly and a renewed whiff of his oakmoss scent drifted on an errant breeze in her direction. When had she ever been so curious about cologne? Usually it gave her a headache, but the subtle scent of oakmoss teased her closer to him, even encouraged a deeper breath. Her shoulder brushed his again. Heat flushed from her neck to her cheeks. What on earth was wrong with her?

"He was duly warned about your decisive nature."

Quiet greeted them again, as the tip-tap of rain and the clip of her shoes kept time together.

"I'm glad you don't want to become involved. It's a good choice for you."

His words pinched at her frayed nerves. Did he think she couldn't manage the challenges? Had he heard about her previous appointment? Her failure? "Have you had a change of heart then? Or was my argument to not join sufficient enough to change your mind?" She hesitated, formulating her next words to drive home the next point. "Unless you doubt my abilities."

She'd expected a glare or maybe a humored grin, but his brow furrowed much like his father's had when speaking of miracles. Something quaked awake inside of her chest. What was that expression?

"Working at the college allows you to do something you love to do. Making a name for yourself and other women." He kept his face forward, their pace slowing. "And you're safe there. It's where you should stay."

She slid him a glance from her periphery, his acknowledgement the proverbial last straw for her pretzeled emotions of the evening. "You forfeited the right to tell me what to do when you stopped being my friend."

He drew in a deep breath but didn't turn. "I've never stopped being your friend. "You..." He paused their walk and shook his head, searching for something to say.

She'd waited three years. She could certainly wait until he found the words. Perhaps, they would finally provide the answer she somehow needed to know.

"You never had time anymore."

Definitely not worth the wait. "Time? Three years ago my time became my mother's property as she delved into a disastrous expedition to catch me a husband. All my time was hers and hers alone. She was a madwoman about it all."

He squinted his blue eyes at her. "What?"

Surely, he'd seen her mother's exploits. Recognized the rabid approach Clarissa Rakes took toward matrimony for her children. Hadn't he? "Mother took hold of my schedule and, at first, planned tea after tea with one eligible man after another. She finally chose Richard for me, announcing to the whole world we were engaged when I'd not approved at all. The man smelled of hair oil and was only truly married to polo." She grimaced. "Horses are lovely creatures, but... polo?" She frowned, recalling her ex-fiancé's fondness for hitting balls with mallets while astride a horse. "When she started planning the wedding without my consent, I had to stop her. Richard's interest in another woman sped up the dissolution of the engagement and he left." She stared at Christopher, searching his face, her throat tickling. "But so did you. You fit so nicely into my life by popping in or sending notes. You understood me, as...as no one but Charlie ever has. And then...and then, the notes grew fewer and finally stopped altogether."

"I didn't fit into your new life, Livy. You never had time to see me. Notes were my only way to keep some semblance of a connection with you, but then..." He crushed a hand over his hair. "I suppose I felt unimportant...then replaced...and you never tried to bridge the gap to find me." He groaned. "It sounds so pitiful when I say it aloud."

"Replaced?" What on earth was the man thinking! Perhaps he wasn't insightful enough to be a clever spy after all. "I can't replace you.

Believe me, I've tried. The only filling I've found close enough is resentment, and I don't like the taste of it at all."

He stared at her, shifting his attention from her eyes to her lips to her hair, as if they were important to him. She attempted not to like the feeling of his gaze searching hers, but her usual self-control failed. "I never stopped being your friend, Livy."

She swallowed and set her chin, refusing to allow this softening feeling in her chest to spread to her very sensible mind. "But I..." She looked toward the sky. "I'm not certain I'm willing to be yours."

"Why...why not?"

Her breaths took on a life of their own, forced one after another as she recalled with clarity the memory of those first few months without him. "You don't understand. You left. You were as constant in my life as my parents. You were my confidante, my companion." A strange fire stung her eyes, and she cleared her throat in a most unladylike way. "Then you were gone. I couldn't function. I was empty inside, listless. It was horrible." Her gaze shot to his wide-eyed one. "I cried."

"You cried?" His whisper echoed to her in disbelief.

"Tears." She pointed to her face. "Dripping off my nose, for one day, maybe two. I try not to remember. It was very uncomfortable."

"You...you never cry."

"Which is why I cannot risk renewing something that could possibly alter my world again to such an extent. I'd never...never felt so much at one time in my entire life."

"I thought you were to be married so I...I stepped out of the way."

"Why should marriage end our friendship?" Heat seared her vision, and the foreign tingle in her nose almost sent her sneezing. *No! Crying again?* She glared at Christopher, who was clearly the cause of such discomfort. "Were you truly so shallow as that?"

Her accusation failed to distance him. In fact, he stepped closer.

"Livy." His voice took on a softness that somehow penetrated her hurt, her anger. The way his voice cradled her name, beckoned her, tingled with a request...a gentleness too confusing to comprehend. "I didn't know I mattered so much to you."

She stared at him as if he were the daftest man in all of England. How could he not have known? No one took up more of her time during her childhood than Christopher Dawson. They'd studied physics and literature together, argued through differing philosophies, and written letters to one another throughout school. No one outside of her family had impacted her life with such acute influence. He'd mattered. Infinitely mattered. "You're having me on."

"You referred to me as fixture, Livy."

"And?"

His lips softened into a smile. "And I thought you were choosing everything except me. I had no idea you were completely unaware of how your distance, your perceived indifference, impacted me." He shifted a step closer, stealing her clarity with oakmoss. "I think we both misunderstood."

All her focus settled onto his eyes, and though her head didn't fully understand the look he gave her, her heart seemed to respond by drawing her closer.

"Livy, I beg your forgiveness, and I very much want you to be my friend." His whisper breathed over her cheeks, sending tingles down her arms and butterflies into her stomach. They wanted the same thing, but the definition of friendship blurred into something different than before.

Some intangible desire she tiptoed toward.

A horn blared into the moment.

Livy blinked, her thoughts reclaiming her usual sensibilities instead of dissolving into whatever magnetism drew her too him.

The horn sounded again. "Christopher." Captain Dawson drove up in his tourer, his head out the window. "We've been called into the office."

Office? A war crisis?

Christopher opened his mouth then closed it again, his brow pinched in a series of wrinkles. He pushed the umbrella into her hand. "For the rain."

"I'm only a door down."

His lips tipped to one side. "And you need a brolly." He doffed his hat and slipped into his father's car, leaving her feeling much less in control of her emotions than she'd been before dinner.

She really didn't want to like Christopher Dawson.

CHAPTER 4

Livy rounded her desk in her small office at University College and reigned in her uncharacteristically distracted mind from ruminating about Christopher Dawson's words and actions. His peculiar behavior uprooted all sorts of unexpected questions and feelings in her. Why had her busyness wounded him so much that he disappeared from her life? For that matter, what reason would spur him to react so rashly? She tugged at the collar of her button-up. And had he intended to kiss her in the rain last night?

"Was the paper so bad, Miss Rakes?"

Livy blinked at the paper in her hands then to the young student seated in a chair across from her desk. Poor Emmalee Langston looked positively horrified.

Livy relaxed her stance by sitting on the corner of her desk, hoping the changed posture offered an easier approach. "You're a fine writer. Better than most of the class, actually. But, you must become the very best to be noticed and make any mark, Miss Langston."

The young woman took the marked paper with a frown. "Why is that?"

Livy crossed her arms, wondering how long it would take for the sheltered young woman to face the harsh reality of changing times and attitudes of thought. "We've made great strides since the first war in showing our skills and abilities, but until women are seen for what we can do, we'll always have to work harder to prove it. It is the way of the world."

"Like you've done, Miss Rakes? A woman in this unique position at the college?"

Livy tamed a smile. "Times are changing, Emmalee, and I hope you'll do much better than me, perhaps achieve full professorship, even. The signs all point to the inevitable future of the first woman to achieve such recognition at this school. You have the brain for it. All you need is a bit more courage. Take the chance to be bold and show what you can do." She tapped the paper in Emmalee's hands. "My notes are a challenge, not a death knell. You can choose whether your mistakes lead you to giving up or..." Her words took hold of her, sinking into her with a shudder of clarity. "Going forward stronger than before."

Like joining the OSE? The thought slipped into her psyche like a whisper but left a gaping hole of questions. Had she given up because of her mistakes?

"Miss Rakes?"

Livy stiffened her lips into a smile. "When you return to school from holiday, keep that in mind, will you?"

Emmalee stood, breathing in the challenge. "Yes, ma'am. I will."

"Excellent. Enjoy your break, Miss Langston, and do be kind to your younger brother. He has quite a legacy to live up to following you into school."

The young woman's grin beamed brighter and her posture lengthened as she exited the room.

Livy eased into her desk chair, absorbing the silence of the school at the end of a session. Dense books filled cases lining the walls of her office, almost shading the one large window from sunlight. One of her two master's degrees hung on the wall next to a reproduction of Rembrandt's *Philosopher in Meditation*.

She studied the work as she'd done many times, the aged man sitting in repose, light haloing him amidst the surrounding darkness. What was the philosopher considering? Was he praying? Waiting?

For what?

And the symbolism of the light... Was it faith? Understanding? Courage?

Did the philosopher wish to connect with the woman tending the fire in the shadows of the room? Reach out to the only other human present in the painting?

For being blessed with such an accurate memory, Livy had taken much too long to understand the more nuanced and intricate world of relationships. She still felt lost most of the time. Details, facts, rote responses, and learning social expectations had come quickly, a set of patterns in behavior, but in understanding deeper emotions and reading people with accuracy, she still teetered half-in-shadow. Clearly, based on her conversation with Christopher, she still had much to learn—about relationships and herself. What was he saying without words?

If she were going to encourage students to shore up their bravery and fight against the tyranny of the day, shouldn't she lead by example? She'd prayed for guidance in church on Sunday, a sliver of doubt in her refusal rousing her decision to accept Captain Dawson's dinner invitation. But how could she take the risk again?

The usual welcome in her quiet office resounded with accusation instead. Christopher's words about her needing to stay where she was bit at her conscience like a challenge. What had she just told Emmalee? To have courage? To take a chance?

Her heart squeezed against her own exhortation. A halo of late morning sunlight graced the room with a gentle glow and turned her attention toward the window, autumn colors brightening the view of stone buildings with vibrant golds, reds, and oranges. Livy sighed.

I'm not brave enough to fail again, God.

The quiet needled deeper, a nail picking at her excuses. God had given her the gift of languages. No other explanation fit the ease with which she learned them. Then there was her delight and almost obsessive curiosity in observation. Her initial training with the OSE had bolstered her confidence. She'd finished near the top of her group of trainees, proving she had what was needed...until she'd failed. Hadn't she failed at enough? An unmarried disappointment to her mother. A woman unable to attain professorship despite her scholarly works. And a failed agent whose indecisiveness led to another person's death.

A sudden weariness pressed her face into her palms. Her head accused, nudging her to step beyond her failures and use her skills to battle against this war, to be as brave as her brother. But her heart? Oh, her heart ached for the life lost at her hands and the fear she'd fail again, branding her as weak as the unvoiced accusations from everyone around her.

Oh God, what would you have me do?

"Miss Rakes, I'm sorry to disturb you."

Christopher!

Livy turned toward the door as Christopher entered the room, looking smart in a navy suit and dark brown fedora. He pulled the office door closed behind him without invitation, his cerulean eyes blazing into her with urgency. She stood, every fiber of her skin raised to awareness.

Something was wrong.

"Livy."

She braced her arms across her chest, readying for the blow. "What is it?" His expression spiked her fear and drew her around the desk. "Christopher. Chris— Mr. Dawson. What?"

He slid his hat from his head and reached into his jacket to retrieve a slip of paper. "You know how Father and I were called unexpectedly away last evening?"

"Yes."

His gaze never left hers as he crossed the space to stand before her. "Two more planes were downed over France within the week."

All heat whooshed from her body, and her fingers dug into her arms.

"Charlie's was one of them."

She reached behind her for the desk, clutching its ledges as she made her way to the chair behind it. Colors, questions, and confusion crashed through her mind. Her attention clung to Christopher's, half in disbelief and half in hope.

"Is he…"

"We received word early this morning that he's been taken prisoner, but you're not supposed to know that."

She breathed out her held breath. *Alive.*

"This is what your family should know."

With trembling hands, she reached for the telegram he held out to her.

THE SECRETARY OF WAR DESIRES ME TO EXPRESS HIS DEEP REGRET THAT YOUR SON SERGEANT CHARLES P. RAKES HAS BEEN REPORTED MISSING IN ACTION OVER FRANCE SINCE OCTOBER 5. LETTER FOLLOWS.

"I'm sorry, Livy."

Her thoughts began to reorder, to comprehend, to solve. She needled Christopher with a stare. "What do you know?"

He sighed and took a seat across from her, placing his hat in his lap. "Not much." His fingers trailed through his hair, upsetting the pale mass. "His plane went down over western France, in some of the least friendly territory. We've received communication that the surviving pilots were taken as prisoners, and it's my hope Charlie was one of them."

"A prisoner in occupied France?" She ran a hand over her face and slipped into the chair next to Christopher. "Does that mean we wait for a prisoner exchange, or worse, the war's end before we know if he survived?"

His hesitation deepened Livy's already plummeting concern. "Is he a lost cause, Christopher? Tell me plainly."

"I don't consider any of those men lost causes, dead or alive. They're all heroes." The conviction in his words brought her eyes back to his stormy blue ones. He leaned closer, checking over his shoulder to the door before continuing. "I happen to have a particular interest, however, in finding lost aviators. It's become one of my specialties, you may say. That I'm still alive is a testament to Providence, a good team, and a few wits. but if anyone can find them, it's my team."

So that was his assignment in this war. He rescued people. The thought failed to inspire a witty response. He'd always been the sort.

Standing up to bullies, running after escaped dogs, blocking the harsh words of the boys at school who'd ridiculed Livy for years because of her odd, bookish ways. Another piece of the Christopher puzzle clicked into place and softened her to him in a new way. Or maybe, not so new but...understood?

"Is that a similar position your father wanted for me?"

He nodded. "It's the more dangerous of operatives. We're out on the field, walking among the enemy, and many times we're exposed to whatever may come. It takes shrewd observation skills and cool intellect in the face of the unexpected and dangerous. High emotion is a liability. Objectivity is invaluable."

She studied the man before her, noting the confidence in the tilt of his jaw. "So you can find him, you think?"

"I don't know." His gaze fastened on hers. "But I'll do whatever is in my power to bring him home."

"Alive."

He nodded. "Alive."

The silence pressed in around her, accusations rising through the noiseless air with the force of a scream. She could help them. But the fear rallied to the defense. Is that why he came to her? A ploy to convince her to join? Her breath hinged and the cool realization of being fooled again chilled the heat rising in her cheeks. She pressed her palms against the arms of the chair and pushed herself up, holding his gaze. "Are you using my brother's predicament to coerce me to join?"

He shot to his feet. "Don't place me in one of your boxes, Livy." She slid a step away from the force in his voice. "Your brother has been my friend as many years as you. If you knew me at all, you'd know I'd never manipulate your feelings. Never." He smashed his hat onto his head and turned for the door. "When I saw his name on the telegram, I came to you before sharing this news with your parents. I sought your guidance, not your compromise or ridicule. I know your mother's condition...her emotional frailty."

All fight fled from Livy's body. The fog of her suspicions began to clear with the sting of shame. She sighed and pressed her fingers into her forehead. "I'm sorry, Christopher." A breath of silence passed before he turned from the door to face her again. "I spoke out of fear. Forgive me?"

He took a few steps closer, and her awareness of his nearness unfurled an overwhelming longing she'd never experienced. She *wanted* his comfort. His care.

She'd recognized the apparent sweetness in a touch or an embrace that others enjoyed, but not until this uncertain moment had she ever desired—no, craved—to be a recipient. Her family had never been the affectionate sort. Her mother kept to a respectable social distance, even in the privacy of their home, and her father's gregarious nature effused a distant sort of kindness but rarely included more than a pat to the cheek. But Christopher's world boasted such affection and tenderness. His parents exuded welcome and comfort, a magnetism and familial trait held by their son. Even as children, Christopher and his sister inspired her curiosity with their warmth—a warmth now tempting to pour over the chill the telegram left behind.

She wasn't alone.

Her watery gaze flickered to his. Tugged closer toward the compassion she saw, her heart offered silent entreaty.

He answered her call and cupped her shoulders with his palms, steadying her. "I...I realize this is painful, Livy, but there's hope. We have a strong team with connections all over France. We'll find him, but it may take time."

Painful. Terrifying. His words barely grazed the surface of the dissonance circulating within her chest but somehow worked their tender wonders, a sweet memory from long ago piercing deeply beneath the pretense and self-honed expectations.

"We can't tell my parents. Not yet. Father's heart isn't strong..." Livy stared at the telegram. "And Mother cannot manage it."

He nodded, his gaze flipping from the wretched telegram to her face. "What would you have me do, Livy?"

Her name pearled from his lips on a breath, the gentleness of it as tactile as a touch. She curled the telegram into her fist and firmed her jaw, accepting her fate. "Allow me to help you, Mr. Dawson. Allow me to help you find my brother."

CHAPTER 5

"Emery said our newest addition is a crack shot."

Christopher looked away from the recent supply delivery to his father's approach. In only a few days into training, Livy had made a name for herself with her expert marksmanship and keen understanding of the protocol. Christopher had never doubted her ability to meet the external challenges of their field, but he couldn't remove the memory of fear in Livy's eyes when she'd learned of Charlie's disappearance. Nor the look of determination that sealed her decision to rejoin the OSE. Keeping the head above the heart in this line of work proved a survival skill, and with Livy on his team, his heart was becoming too entrenched.

He should never have approached her with the news of Charlie's situation. It was Christopher's fault she was here—the last place he wanted her to be.

"She's not lost any of her previous skill."

Christopher granted his father a begrudging nod. There was something to be said for her uncanny ability to focus. A natural skill. Her cool, calculated personality fit perfectly into the world of espionage. He frowned. Despite his desire to sever his emotional ties to her, each new encounter with her only tightened them. For heaven's sakes, he'd almost kissed her.

He gritted his teeth against the mental acknowledgement. *And he still wanted to.* "Not everyone with skills belongs in service, Father. She's new to our particular operatives."

"But they're not incredibly different than the other departments. I've no doubt she has the wits and the determination to sort it all out in record time. Remarkable." Father moved beside him and picked up the pipe pistol, oblivious to Christopher's hesitation. "You know, we've placed the suicide pills in the handle of your pipe now instead of in the back of your cigarette case. Several agents have been discovered with the cigarettes."

Christopher toyed with a tube of lipstick, gliding expert fingers over the smooth vile until his nail caught on a hinge. With a careful touch, the base of the tube opened to reveal a tiny knife. "This is new."

"Necessity is the mother of invention, yes?" Father took the tube from his hands and clipped the knife inside its casing. "Another radio operator was captured. Our women need more means of protection. This is a first tool of many to ensure their safety."

Safety? Talking Livy into joining the SOE started as a simple challenge from his father, but now? Now his doubts resurrected with a fury. She'd appeased her parents with some story about how her university position requested research on the cultural shift of women in the war effort, sending her to southern England to investigate French-English mindsets and relationships, but Christopher had seen her vulnerability.

"I appreciate her skills, Father, but I stand behind my first thoughts about Miss Rakes. We are placing her on a high-level mission when she's only started as an operative."

"Nonsense. She worked for a year in an internal department of the OSE not even six months ago."

"And did you find out why she left them?"

"Personal reasons. Nothing to do with her abilities."

Christopher placed his palms against the table, chin set with his decision. "If you're determined to place her then she's on my team, Captain."

His father's brows rose to his hairline. "Are you certain she wouldn't be a distraction for you?"

Christopher leveled his father with a stare. "It will be more of a distraction if she isn't with me." He lowered his voice. "No one will attempt to keep her safer than I will."

Gravity settled into his father's expression. "No, I should think not."

"But I'm still not certain she's the right fit for this mission." Christopher examined a coat with a medical kit sewn into the lining, searching for another excuse to keep Livy from crossing into France. "It wasn't three weeks ago that she rejected any interest in the cause. How can we be certain she's committed?"

"I'm committed."

Christopher turned to the sound of Livy's voice, but the woman staring at him didn't match the image he'd expected. Gone was the tight-fitted bun and gray suit. Instead, the stylist had conformed Livy's dark hair to curl at her shoulders in the latest fashion, bringing out her auburn highlights. Her white collared shirt buttoned to the ruffled top, and a skirt met her small waist at the band, cinching her curves until the fabric flared at the knee in a colorful pink.

He'd never noticed how shapely she was. His throat constricted. He noticed now.

The most fascinating enhancement came from her eyes. Whatever magic the agents and instructors worked behind those closed doors, Christopher couldn't sort out how they'd made Livy's eyes appear even larger and darker. Paired with those stark red lips, he couldn't pull his gaze from her face.

No, England was where Livy Rakes needed to stay.

"We wouldn't wish for you to feel forced into this, Livy." His father's words emerged into Christopher's periphery. "You're placing your future, your very life, at stake, you know."

"I've been through all of the information, Captain, and I am well-aware of the risks."

Christopher blinked at her response, his brain matching the familiar, clipped voice with the fashionable beauty before him. "I see your session with Miss Porter was successful."

Her brilliant gaze flung to his. "Successful? Is that what it's called? She picked me apart like a biological specimen and left me looking more like a clown than a person."

Her eyes brightened, highlighting the faintest ribbon of gold encircling her pupils. Intelligence and fury proved a magnetizing combination. He pulled at his collar and looked away, breaking the curious enchantment.

"Don't you dare smile at my misery, Christopher Dawson. You have no earthly idea of the utter scorn to which I've been subjected." Even with the fierce turn of her brows, a faint hint of humor softened her lips. "The woman preached for an hour on the ritualistic act of applying cosmetics. Not to mention the lengths she took to lecture me about my hairstyle." Livy's hand flew up to match the passion in her words. "This from a middle-aged woman who will not admit she hails from Lincolnshire, possibly Grimsby, and has at least one parent of German descent, judging from her physical features, accent, and name."

Christopher's smile widened against his will. The old Livy still held court beneath this enhanced beauty. And she did look beautiful. More than ever, which didn't bode well for his recovering heart. At all.

"And the red lipstick does nothing for her complexion at all. I told her so, and I suppose that's why she forced me into this detestable piece of frivolity. Oh, to be a man!" She waved toward the skirt. Her expectant expression took an uncertain turn. "Why are you staring at me like that?"

It took a moment for him to locate his voice. "The cosmetics are...new."

"And bothersome. There are rules for every possible application! How to rub the cream just so, the proper amount of mascara, and the exact specifics of lining my lips with a perfect color to match my nails." Her pink fingertips pressed into her forehead and she sighed. "It's preposterous. My lips stand out like a beacon."

Yes, they did. Christopher cleared his throat and turned his face from hers. Distractingly so.

"And then there's the hair and the clothes. Evidently the flared skirt is the style in France as opposed to the more sensible pencil skirt." She waved her hand to the pink skirt that did absolutely nothing to hide the delicate curves of her legs. "I'm as frothy as a peony." She groaned. "I smell like one too. How do women manage this sort of superficiality on a regular basis? It's a perfect waste of an hour. Do you realize how much useless information I have in my head now?"

Christopher couldn't catch his chuckle in time.

She zeroed in on him. "Christopher Dawson, how dare you laugh when I'm clearly out of sorts?"

He leaned closely to breathe in the peony scent, a fragrance that did not match Livy Rakes at all. "It's not a waste."

Her brow tilted ever so slightly, challenging him. "Is that so?"

"You look beautiful, Livy."

Those stormy eyes widened then wavered into cool indifference, a feature she'd perfected since he'd left England. "Thank you. A worthy disguise then, don't you think?"

"I was glad to hear you hadn't lost your skills, Miss Rakes." His father broke into the conversation. Christopher's old surge of protection, the natural pull of her intelligence and wit, the need to delve beyond her stoicism and uncover the gentle, compassionate soul beneath resurrected as the wounds from the past peeled away as thin as paper. Blast his soft heart. It had always belonged to Olivia Rakes.

He captured his wayward thoughts with the steady hand of profession. Time to don his own mask for now, but with her external beauty matching her natural beauty of mind, he'd have his own challenge in keeping his indifference checked.

"It seems I'm well suited for espionage and repulsing men, Captain." Her grin took a challenging turn. "Having second thoughts on your choice?"

"Not one wit of doubt. And if you keep to this schedule, we should be able to send you out within the week." A twinkle danced to life in Christopher's father's eyes. "Though, Livy, your next session...or two... is going to be on interpersonal relations and reading them with more clarity."

Christopher raised a warning brow at his father.

"I do feel as though I miss certain nuances in relationships that others understand, but you'll be pleased to know I can probably shoot my way out of a misunderstanding of nonverbal communication should it be necessary."

His father raised a hand over his mouth to cover his poorly disguised laugh. Christopher hoped Livy's misunderstanding of nonverbal communication extended to the lapse in judgment on the former sea captain's part, accidental or not.

"Perhaps, it would be wise to reconsider going to the field immediately. Further your training in interpersonal skills, sharpen your understanding of the dynamics of our particular department?" Christopher followed her to the counter with the newest espionage devices on display in the room, away from his father and the other agents. He cringed as she chose a lip gloss case with a secret compartment in the bottom to hide the suicide pills. "If you are…uncertain at all."

Her gray eyes shot to his. "Agent Atkins and your father both feel I'm prepared. But you seem to doubt my abilities altogether."

"No, you are quite capable of anything you set your mind to, Livy."

Her jaw tightened. "Then you *do* think it's hopeless to search for Charlie?"

He shook his head. "No, in fact, intel provided information that Charlie's been confined in a chateau occupied by a Commandant Wolfe."

"He's alive," she whispered then looked to him. "What will happen to him there?"

Beneath her steady voice, the pretentious strength, her gaze wavered. *Livy, don't come with me.*

"He could remain there indefinitely, be moved to one of the camps, or…"

She nodded, her nails fisting into her palm. "And there are others like him?"

"Livy, listen to me. I've lost friends, colleagues, and fellow agents during my years in the OSE. I…I think perhaps it would be best if you worked in our department here."

She placed the lipstick tube onto the counter and leveled him with her undivided attention. "You're afraid I'm not strong enough to complete this mission? You have no faith in me?"

He ran his hand through his hair, working an answer he didn't understand. "No, it's not that."

"You don't like me enough to partner with me?"

That wasn't the problem at all. "Of course I like you."

"I thought you were above the discrepancy of our sexes."

He shot her a stare that stilled her tongue. "Truly, you think that? Of me?" He stepped closer, holding her gaze and watching those fathomless eyes grow wider. "I'm on *your* side, Livy, whatever side that may be. If anyone wants you to succeed, to outlast this mission, this war, it's me."

Her gaze wavered in his, asking questions, confused.

His volume faltered. "I...I don't want to lose you again."

"Lose me?" She blinked. "Again?"

He inwardly scolded himself and turned toward the door, cramming his hat on his head. "It doesn't matter." How could he have allowed her to break his resolve? "I must prepare. We leave in five days."

SHE'D NOT SEEN CHRISTOPHER FOR DAYS. HER PARACHUTE TRAINING and myriad other exercises to shore up her previously learned skills kept her engaged, but an undercurrent of curiosity about him niggled through her waking hours.

It had taken her two days to piece together some explanation of his statement about losing her *again*. Answers to some clever questions to Agent Atkins during her sessions on interpersonal communication and the subterfuge of "charming" information out of her targets provided Livy a clearer picture of Christopher's behavior ...along with a sliver of dawning. He cared about her.

He'd always cared about her.

In such a way, he battled against the pain of it.

And she'd never truly realized until now. Would she have understood his meaning if he had been more demonstrative, or had she truly been so engrossed in her studies and the tedious occupation of having a fiancé that she wouldn't have recognized his affection? Everything else came with such clarity to her mind, such relative ease. Why not relationships, especially matters of the heart?

"Here's your information. Your code name is Constance, alias Constance Moreau." Agent Atkins dropped a packet of paper on the table in front of Livy. "You are paired with Agent Dawson and leave on Wednesday."

One of the other agents had mentioned that the renowned agent Vera Atkins occasionally visited the country estate now used for training, but Livy hadn't dared hope to meet the mysterious spymistress. She embodied so much of what Livy idolized. Independent, strong, and respected by her male comrades. In a world where women of like-intellect were not allowed to hold tenure at university, Vera Atkins shone as a beacon of possibility—even if her beacon glowed in a covert direction.

"We have three teams who will be dropped at three different landing sites in France. Each team is to gather intel on the welfare and location of our pilots. If the situation allows and your team members agree, you will then attempt to rescue the airmen." She tapped the paper. "Your contact in France is Camille Baudin."

Livy shot her attention to Agent Atkins. "There is an actress by that name."

Agent Atkins's red lips twitched. "She would be the same. Don't look so surprised, Miss Rakes. Our people come from all walks of life and all professions with one goal—ending this war. There are actors, musicians, politicians, and businessmen. World-renowned pianist Amelia Rippey has worked with us for almost a year."

"She's American. America is not a part of this war."

"Yet." Agent Atkins's brow rose. "The scope of this war has already stretched far beyond what anyone could have imagined and with no end in sight. We need any faithful soul and quick mind we can get."

"I'm ready to do my part." Livy stood without hesitation. "You've prepared me well."

Agent Atkins studied Livy with hawk-like acuity to such an extent that Livy's skin prickled. "I feel certain you can convince anyone that you are French and easily escape handcuffs or burgle a house." She crossed her arms, eyes narrowing with deeper scrutiny. "But you are entering a world where any minute anomaly puts you at risk of being under the Germans' watch, or worse, under their thumbs. The smallest things betray you. An exclamation of surprise in English, a wrong tilt of your hat, ordering black coffee." Her gaze penetrated Livy's calm, knifing her with warning. "You must *become* two people living in one body. The outer shell is Constance to the finest detail, and the inner core must remain the alert spy. Olivia Rakes and her emotions, history..." She tilted her head. "Family cannot become a distraction. You must separate feeling from this assignment. Sincere emotions have no place in the world of espionage. Save it for novels and the home front, not here. You are on the field now."

Agent Atkins walked out of the room, but Livy took her challenge to heart. If she was going to separate feeling from the assignment, she'd better sort this matter of her heart and Christopher Dawson's before they crossed into occupied France.

CHAPTER 6

He wouldn't look at her. They'd spent almost an hour in awkward silence as the Lysander hummed toward France, and Christopher had barely spoken a word. Of course, cramped quarters surely contributed to Christopher's silence—the packed plane held just enough space for two agents, a pilot, and a dispatcher—and, of course, she shouldn't concern herself with the unanswered personal questions regarding her and Christopher's relationship, as Agent Atkins had advised. But...well, she needed her mind clear to focus on the mission, and the only way to do that was to settle this needling curiosity.

The tight space gave her ample opportunity to study him afresh. All the darkness of war and death led a person to seek hope, and this newfound awareness of Christopher beamed with something grounded despite the turmoil around them. He was handsome, intelligent, resourceful...but more than that, his friendship painted her youth with a glow of something sweet and tender, a genuine care. Something she wanted to capture in a new way, like the light in her Rembrandt.

"We should get some rest while we can." Christopher called over the sound of the engine and moved toward a small empty space in the back of the plane, all but disappearing into the shadows. "Once we jump, there's no knowing how quickly we'll need to evacuate the landing field or how long it may take to arrive at the nearest safe house." He rolled out a sleeping bag onto the narrowed floor and gestured toward it, keeping his focus on his work. "Rest will help keep our wits about us."

"How many jumps have you made?" She stood, grabbing a nearby hand-hold as the plane shuddered with a bout of turbulence. The parachute jumpsuit covering her civilian clothes reduced her fluidity of movement, and the blacked-out windows nearly made it impossible to see very far in front of her. Boxes holding their supplies, particularly the coveted Oreka, lay in wait to trip her as she moved from one steadying cloth-grip to the next.

"Six." He rolled out another bag next to the first.

"And were they all uneventful?"

His attention shot to her for a second then returned to the bags. "Five of them were. I lost my partner on the third jump."

He knew loss too, and yet, he continued. Bravery was an appealing trait in a partner, romantic or otherwise. The plane shuddered again, sending her slightly off balance. Christopher's hand found hers in the dark, providing support and gentle guidance in the narrow space they'd share for sleep. Her pulse took on an increased rhythm, and her fingers remained in his even when she'd reached the sleeping bags, reluctant to release his hold. What a strange and interesting development!

"Your first time on a plane?" He tugged her the remaining steps.

"That obvious?"

The white of his eyes flickered in the gray light. "A little." His palms moved to her shoulders as he lowered her to her bag. "I placed loose money in your jacket pocket before we left headquarters."

"Thank you." She slid into the bag and adjusted the cloth around her. "And I've familiarized myself with our contact, Camille Baudin. I communicated with her before we left headquarters. She's expecting us in two days."

"Excellent."

"From my research, I have a feeling Mademoiselle Baudin is going to prove quite the personality."

Even in the shadows his grin tilted, and for some odd reason, her attention hesitated on his lips. A raw and surprisingly delightful warmth glowed under her skin, rose up her neck, and flushed her cheeks. The world had afforded her many experiences but never true romance. Her fiancé filled a social expectation arranged by her parents, but this...this gravitating interest held her, awakening something untouched.

Christopher had called her beautiful.

"I believe you're right, but she has proven indispensable to the cause and lethal in the protection of both British and French." He leaned close to her, zipping her pack to her neck. His voice swooped low, brightening the inner glow. "You're ready for this, Livy. I know you are."

Her breath squeezed around her reply. "I'm flattered."

"Flattered, is it?"

She pulled another breath through her tightening throat. "That I've found a way to impress you, Agent Dawson."

His fingers stalled on the zipper at her neck, the rise and fall of his chest hinting the increase of his breathing wasn't just from anxiety over their upcoming mission. Could it be from their closeness? How had she never noticed? "You've never failed to leave an impression, Miss Rakes."

He turned and slipped into the neighboring sleeping bag. The rumble of the engine growled into the silence as he settled down, the effect of his closeness tangible and curious.

"Christopher?"

The bag shifted beside her, nudging the faintest hint of oakmoss her way. "Yes, Livy."

The smile in his words sparked her own. No, this swirling warmth igniting her deepest emotions shone with a different hue than mere friendship. Or perhaps it shone the same hue in a richer shade. Yes, this tender familiarity branched out from something familiar into something new.

"What did you mean a few days ago?"

"We've had several discussions in recent days. Are you referring to the one about burying our parachutes once we land or the proximity of the nearest safe house or—"

"When you mentioned losing me again."

He hesitated so long that she tilted her face in his direction. His profile pointed toward the ceiling. "I spoke too rashly then."

"You spoke from your heart, and I'd appreciate clarification."

He released an audible sigh into the silence. "You want to have this conversation *now*? When we're on a plane over occupied France?"

"Clearly it should have happened three years ago, so I'd appreciate not prolonging its tardiness further." A puff of frustration burst from her nose, and she looked up at the ceiling. "Besides, we're both trapped here for the present, and I daresay sleep is a distant hope at best. Nonexistent for me, with this particular mystery."

Silence moved through the shadows, inciting her pulse into an unwelcome gallop. "So, unless you wish to hear of my latest research on the linguistic complexities of Gaelic, or worse, a recitation on the ritual of applying cosmetics, I suggest you loosen your tongue and duly kill my aching curiosity."

"Men and women rarely speak so bluntly of anything, especially romance. It's...not done."

"Come now, Christopher. I've made it a point in my life to do what is not done. Why should I shy away now?" Her throat scratched dry. The threat of his denial pulsed against her bold declaration, calling her bluff. His interest and his opinion mattered to her more than ever. In a way carved deep enough to change her life. "And...and I don't understand you. I feel...I feel an unsettling between us, and if we are to renew our friendship then I want—"

"Our friendship, of course." He cleared his throat.

She braced herself, stepping over the precipice into worlds unknown. "Or something more?"

Another swell of silence met her challenge, her freefall. She could feel his gaze on her profile, could almost visualize the intense turn of his cerulean eyes. There was no safety net where she'd plunged. Her breath held.

"Once your mother sets her mind to something, she moves with the speed of a cheetah." He chuckled in the dark, not a particularly happy sound but one that held a hint of sadness. "I suppose that's where part of your tenacity comes from."

"I hope I can improve upon any obstinance I've inherited."

She didn't see his smile, but she felt it, drawing her into his camaraderie. "I'd barely recognized my feelings when you were suddenly engaged to Desmond Cork."

The name sounded as attractive on Christopher's lips as was the man himself. Stiff, arrogant, and enamored with his new money.

"Your feelings?" She doubted he heard her whispered question over the sound of the plane's engine.

"I…well, you became engaged to the wrong man. That is, I thought you had."

Her mind whirled, a sudden shift in her memories taking on this new information, replaying scenes from their last encounters before he'd disappeared from her life. The sting of his absence had plagued her these past three years, but she'd never imagined he'd vanished because of her or the pain she'd unintentionally inflicted on him. As her thoughts sifted the memories, the slightest hints emerged. His insistence on walking her home from parties, his gentle questions about her future, the comfort she took in his camaraderie. Heat fled her face. The moment when he'd almost kissed her in the very same closet he'd pinned her in during the benefit.

How had she missed it? But she'd never imagined *him*. In fact, she'd never imagined anyone as a suitor. Desmond had been chosen for her. A mindless acquiesce to the demands of her mother and society.

If she could choose…

"Christopher?"

A pause. He cleared his throat. Did he feel the energy zipping between their silence? Words waiting to be spoken? "Yes, Livy."

"I'm not engaged anymore."

Quiet ensued then a shift in the bag beside her drew her attention. He'd turned his head, staring at her through the shadows and noise, the space between them sparkling with magnetism.

Livy stared back, her breath a shallow substitute for the normal.

"How quickly you forget." His lips bloomed with a hint of a grin. "Well, Constance and Adrien are engaged."

Their aliases were pledged in matrimony, and she'd agreed to play the part.

Her smile released, the connection to him suddenly much stronger, more beautiful. How had she never known? Too focused on the wrong things to see the right ones? "I'm still Livy Rakes and you are still Christopher Dawson until we touch down in France. And I'd like to know what will happen to them." Her breath shivered out, her courage holding tight. "Would you…be willing to try again now that I'm more prepared to see and understand?"

"The game of espionage can take all sorts of unexpected turns. We have an entire mission ahead of us. One of the most dangerous ones I've encountered."

She could play the game too now that her heart understood. "Then I'd advise you, Mr. Dawson, to be more demonstrative in your affections for I will not miss my chance again."

The pilot and dispatcher exchanged words Livy couldn't interpret over the surrounding noise, but she wondered how much time they had left as Livy and Christopher before the façade began. Christopher shifted nearer and a soft warmth touched her temple.

His lips?

She froze. Not that she could move anyway, zipped in from feet to collar bone.

"Livy Rakes." His whisper warmed her ear, and somehow the weight of warmth pressed her eyes closed into a glorious sweetness. She embraced the feelings, the truth. "If we survive this mission, I will ensure that you have no doubt of my affections."

THE FAMILIAR SWOOSH OF AIR AROUND CHRISTOPHER AS HE parachuted to the ground matched the rush inside of him, his heart as suspended as his body. Livy's words shifted everything. She'd opened the door of her heart to him.

If she wanted a demonstrative reaction, let him have fifteen minutes alone with her, and he'd erase any doubt from her mind. He'd dreamed of kissing her for at least a year before her previous engagement to that louse Desmond Cork, and the longings had revived with new energy and old tenderness.

Blast it all, he had to close off his heart. Once his soles touched French soil, the mission needed his undivided focus.

He gripped the straps of his chute and skimmed the dark countryside as it grew closer, moonlight bathing the earth in a haunting glow. Cool air rushed against his face, chilling the skin with the taste of coming-winter. Nothing moved.

Air blustered around him, the thunderous noise in his ears a surprising volume with every jump he made, belying the silence. No animals crossed the verdant hillside. No lavender swayed in the night breeze. All was quiet…and dark.

Where were the reception committees torches?

Livy's parachute took a more westerly direction than his, sending her just beyond the crop of trees to his right. He pulled his cords toward the left, landing a few feet from the trees, and began the speedy process of unlatching his parachute to ensure he had access to his pistol. The darkness seeped through his jumpsuit with the same warning chill during every landing, except this time it bore deeper. Shadows plagued with thick silence and an almost-stilted inertia.

Their plane had arrived later than anticipated, so perhaps the reception committee fell back to safer ground with the intention of returning after another periphery check or two. No one could be too cautious. News of their hastily planned arrival might not have reached their contacts in time, but the stillness unearthed a schism of unease. He scanned the perimeter again, tossed his pack to the side, and detached his parachute, pulling off his gray one-piece with speed and finesse. Dressed in a full navy linen suit, he could be on an evening country stroll with his fiancée without anyone the wiser.

Assuming he could find his fiancée.

He almost grinned at the idea as he gathered his parachute and inventoried their supply packs. One had landed near the tree line and another to the east, both vital to their mission—an Oreka for guiding aircraft to the field and a much-needed wireless. He ran past the packages to the trees, cautious but quick. Partner, first. Packages, after.

Where was Livy?

A rustling of bushes sounded to his right. He slid his pipe pistol from his inside jacket pocket and aimed in the direction. Livy emerged into the fading light, her pale blue suit luminescent in the moon's glow.

"I've started a hole for your chute, but I could use some help."

He resisted the sudden need to take her in his arms and be quite demonstrative indeed. One sentence of hope after years of silence didn't mean immediate romance and certainly not instant kissing. Although a piece of him felt like no time had passed at all. He switched his thoughts into immediate action in a nonromantic direction. Digging. Good distraction.

"I'll finish the job. Would you collect the supply box?" He nodded in the direction of the wireless. "We must get it to the Resistance."

She nodded and moved to pass him, but he caught her arm. "Take care. Our reception committee's gone missing."

"Of course, Monsieur LeCroix." She tacked on a smile with the sound of his alias before moving into the shadows. No, she would not make keeping his mind mission-focused easy at all. He followed her with his gaze until she disappeared, studying the shadows nearby for any movements, any signs. As he dug the shallow hole for their parachutes and jumpsuits to erase any evidence of their landing, the unnerving silence kept his body tense, and one hand close to his pistol.

A sudden shot split through the quiet of the night.

Livy!

Christopher turned toward the trees at a full run, ducking low and taking out his pistol on the way. Livy met him at the tree line, her own pistol drawn. "I've counted three, all German. One older and two younger, I'd guess from the sound of their voices. The breaks in the elder one's speech point to him being somewhat out of shape, I think."

"From which direction?"

"The younger two are to the left of those rocks. The elder is by the forest's edge. He may be out of breath, but he's the crack shot of the lot."

He peeked from around the tree, noting one helmet above a rock outcropping. Three was manageable, at least.

"Do you think they took out our landing party?"

A bullet whizzed past them. He tugged her close to his side, giving her a more solid cover. "It's possible."

Livy fired into the shadows and a cry responded.

Christopher sighted three more men in the moonlight. Six. Thankfully, Christopher and Livy had the advantage of height and cover from their spot, but they were woefully outnumbered and on unfamiliar terrain. Christopher's next shot took out another man. Two down. Four to go.

A bullet zipped by, splintering the bark off a tree to his right.

Christopher turned Livy into him. "You must go on ahead."

"And do what?"

"Go to the safe house. Take the supplies."

Another bullet ricocheted off the tree near Livy. "Don't be ridiculous. You stand a better chance with me here."

He fired a shot at the pair by the rocks and one toppled, but another bullet zipped by their feet. There was more than one crack shot in the lot. Livy and the mission had to come first.

"Livy." He squeezed her arm, his whisper harsh. "I will distract them so you can escape through the wood. We must get the wireless to our contacts, and we can't do that surrounded by the enemy."

She leaned close, her gaze fastened on his, unrelenting. "I'm not leaving you."

"Don't lose sight of the mission. Your brother. Our people on the other side. They need us." Christopher barricaded her with his body as another bullet zipped by. He shook out of his black coat. "This should cloak the paleness of your suit."

Her gaze met his, almost...watery?

"Constance, are you crying?" He used her alias drawing her back to their mission, her ultimate purpose– rescuing her brother.

She growled. "You seem to bring it out in me."

He wrapped his coat around her. "I'd say I'm sorry, but I wouldn't mean it."

She narrowed her eyes at him and fired around his body at the soldiers closing in.

His arms went to her shoulders. "You have your Welbike. It will get you from here faster, but don't turn on the engine until you are out of earshot."

"Christopher, I will not leave you behind—"

"You are not leaving me, I am *choosing* to stay. One of us must make it out of here."

"We'd stand a better chance—"

"Go east toward the safe house as we discussed. If you stay along the tree line, the soldiers will have a harder time tracking you."

"You can't do this alone."

He pushed her behind him, away from the incoming soldiers. "I'll draw them in another direction so you can escape. *I* need you to escape." The admission drew her to a stop. She pinned him with her stare, her eyes almost glowing in the faint light. If she were his last sight on earth, he could die happy.

"I expect you to meet me by morning, Adrien LaCroix. No excuses. I will not lose another fiancé." Her voice caught and softened her words. "Don't disappear again."

Despite the forceful edge in her words, her eyes searched his, speaking words he'd longed to hear from her.

"Then pray for me and go."

Another bullet sailed past them, breaking the moment. "Go. Now."

With one last look at him, she charged toward the wood and Christopher darted in the opposite direction, ready to meet the gunfire and the enemy in the dark.

CHAPTER 7

Livy should have stayed with Christopher. She squeezed her eyes closed and waited in the shadows, offering another prayer for safety. Four hours had passed. *Four.* She'd hopped on her Welbike as soon as she moved out of earshot of the Germans, but the whispers of gunfire still haunted her. She'd failed once again. Memories of her escape from the scene filtered through her mind—the fear, the danger, the uncertainty. *Oh God, please keep Christopher safe!*

A shuffle of noise rustled from outside Livy's hiding place. Concealed in the secret compartment of an old barn, her and Christopher's safehouse for this mission, she drew her pistol from the folds of her jacket and snuffed the lantern light.

For hours the only break in the surrounding silence came from her prayers as memories spliced her resolve, bringing unwelcome tears to her vision. Blasted Christopher Dawson! He'd made her cry twice!

She pinched the gun tight, forcing emotions to bow to cool logic, but her heart pumped a revolt. Focus on the work at hand. Christopher would want this.

And she would succeed for him and Charlie.

The narrow compartment, a lean-to built into the walls of the ramshackle building, measured about four feet wide, but it stretched the length of the barn and held a stockade of emergency supplies. The last person who'd hidden here must have been a woman because a trace of lilac scented the space and remains of heel marks still lodged within the dirt floor. No blood stains or scuffled shoe markings as far as she could see, which meant this hiding spot hadn't been uncovered...yet.

She stepped over a box of canned goods and another of radio parts before reaching the door, pistol at the ready. The tiny peephole, disguised as a knot of the wall board, revealed an empty room. A haze of shadows and lattice of fading moonlight scattered across old hay and unused farm equipment. Nothing moved.

In the distance, brushstrokes of morning gave an otherworldly glow to the dying moonlight. An hour until dawn?

Where was Christopher? Her throat thickened with fresh emotion, but she pushed the tears away, praying instead. Protocol. If Christopher failed to show by dawn, she would move forward. Alone.

That was the agreement should anything happen to one of them.

Constance had to take over now.

An unearthly screech reverberated from the barn door, shattering the silence like a banshee in the dark. A dark, thick figure stepped into view, pistol glistening in the paleness.

Livy's attention zoomed in, blotting out everything else. Feeling. Fear. Failures. Like a camera lens, she took in every detail of the approaching figure. He shuffled, slightly unsteady, though the end of the pistol remained controlled. Wounded, not drunk. His cautious gait edged him farther into the barn, steady but for the slight limp. Ah, not a recent wound.

He held the weapon with confidence and familiarity. Hmm...a soldier, perhaps? Agent?

A sweet hint of tobacco mingled with the dank odor of old hay. Cigar, not cigarette. Paired with the slight bend in the man's walk, Livy placed him outside the typical soldier's age. He stepped closer to the secret door, the confidence in his movements highlighting his intentions. Livy slid against the wall beside the door and prepared for an attack. He'd favored his right side. *Attack the left.*

"Today's not fit for man nor beast."

Livy's shoulders relaxed at the man's use of the secret code in fluent French. With slight hesitation, she replied with a similar fluency, "But at least it's warm and clear."

Through the peephole, Livy watched the man lower his pistol, so she followed suit and waited, her finger taut on the trigger. In war, trust wasn't a commodity. Strangers earned it.

The secret door shook then opened. The man shone his torch and paused as the light hit Livy's face. From the glow, he looked to be her father's contemporary and wore the stern expression of a military man. The Great War, she'd wager. Someone important, most likely.

"I was told there'd be two of you."

Livy turned and relit the lantern, keeping her thoughts distracted. The golden hue spilled into the small compartment, highlighting the stranger wearing farmer's attire and an impassive expression.

"We were ambushed at the drop sight." She refused to give her emotions access to her heart and gestured with her chin toward the supply box on a crate near her feet. "Adrien created a diversion so I could escape with the wireless."

The man studied her then closed the door behind him. "You have the wireless. That will save dozens, if not tens, of lives."

If she hadn't understood the dichotomy of war, his words might have appeared harsh, but he spoke the truth. One wireless message of German movements held massive potential—life-saving potential—though the admission failed to weaken the sting in Christopher's absence.

"Pierre." He held out his hand. She'd heard of his codename. The great saboteur, if rumors proved true. Livy took his hand. "Constance."

He offered a stiff nod of greeting. "I have twenty miles to go to deliver the wireless. Our last operator only lasted three weeks, but our newest girl outlasted her wireless. We hope she'll outlast this one as well."

In his debriefing before the flight, Christopher had shared the vital role of the Resistance's operators and their particular task in passing life-saving information to the team. This operator whom Pierre referred to was the fifth one in six months and had remained alive by changing her location every three to four days to keep the Fritz unaware of her position. They kept relentless watch and had their own spies in every nook in France.

Livy lifted the wireless. "I hope the same."

"For you." Pierre exchanged some papers for the wireless. "New food tickets. Don't use the ones HQ sent with you. The Reich changed them to catch counterfeiters."

"Thank you."

"And prepare yourself for your passage through Rennes to Combourgh." He shifted the wireless beneath his arm and turned toward the door. "The recent Allied bombings have decimated part of the city, and the Germans have increased patrol. You will need to keep on your guard."

Livy's stomach twitched with an added tension. "Thank you for the information."

With another curt nod, he slid from the compartment and into the night. Livy checked her watch. Decisions she'd rather not make but soon must encroached upon her with the approaching dawn. She settled onto an old blanket, snuffed out the lantern, and prayed one last time before drifting into a shallow sleep filled with what-ifs. What if Christopher didn't arrive? What if she had to go on alone?

The softest strum of birdsong awakened her. She drew in a deep breath and stretched to a standing position, attuning her senses to her shadowed surroundings and shaking the fog from her mind. A faint orange glow peeked through the slits in the peephole with an unwelcome reminder.

Christopher wasn't here.

Livy fisted her concern into motion, gathered her supplies, left the compartment, and pulled the Welbike toward the entrance of the barn. The fresh morning air dripped with dew, and a misty fog draped the verdant countryside, revealing a green beauty untouched by bombing raids and gunfire. She tugged Christopher's coat tightly around her shoulders, draping her breath in oakmoss.

Her heart squeezed against returning to the drop off point. Her brother would have told her to turn back, to find Christopher. Christopher would have told her to rescue Charlie. But neither man was with her. Both called to her heart and action. She closed her eyes and drew in a deep breath, recounting the rule forged into her psyche during training. First the mission. *Rescue.*

God help her.

She relinquished her curiosity regarding Christopher's whereabouts, unfolded the Welbike, and secured her supplies in her knapsack before looking one last time to the dark west. A faint ray of sunlight spliced the gray clouds in the distance, falling upon the hilly terrain she'd traveled through last night. Hope?

Let it be so, Lord.

With a final plea to heaven, she turned the bike up the dusty path toward Combourgh.

It was midday before she reached the train station in Liam. People rushed to-and-fro as in any other city, traveling to work or home or on holiday. Only the clipped march of SS troops interwoven throughout the bustling crowd, their black uniforms posing a sense of intimidation from every checkpoint in the station, proved incongruous to the everyday activity of this wounded French city. Double patrol, just as Pierre had said.

After a few appalling glances from passing ladies at, no doubt, her unkempt appearance, Livy took her bags to the toilet to freshen up. Her large eyes stared at her, smudges of mascara darkening the skin underneath her lashes. Her brown hair, highlighted with hints of red, stood to as much attention as her nerves, and whatever lipstick had once graced her lips slanted ever so slightly to the left. She scanned her body.

At least her suit had kept its shape.

Livy replicated with painstaking care the makeup application process she'd been taught and tidied her hair, grimacing so much at her reflection while doing so that her face hurt. What a perfect waste of valuable time, but if she was good at anything, it was imitation.

As she moved to apply the finishing touch of lipstick, her hand shook with such force that the tube quaked in her fingers. She placed her palm against the sink, bracing her weight and slowing her rushed breaths. She'd not planned to travel on alone. Of course, she'd taken the training and understood the possibilities, but this wasn't supposed to happen.

Christopher was supposed to be here too, offering his calming presence, reminding her of the hope buried beneath the uncertainty. She stared at her reflection, the large eyes returning her gaze looking almost vulnerable. No. She shook her head. Too many lives hung on her dedication, to her mission.

Though I walk through the valley of the shadow of death, I will fear no evil.

You are with me.

With or without Christopher, she wasn't alone. She hardened her expression and will, pinching the hand tremor into submission and rubbing the color over her lips.

She emerged from the toilet as pristine as if she'd walked from the OSE offices that morning, and with a steady step, she approached the checkpoint for her train, forcing her nervousness beneath a red-stained smile.

"Your bags and papers, mademoiselle."

Livy held the guard's dark gaze, keeping her grin steady, until his lips softened ever so slightly. "*Bien sur.*" She retrieved her hold on her trunk and handbag.

He rummaged through her handbag, fingering her dreaded cosmetics with the same interest she held, and turned to her trunk. Without any sense of decorum, he opened the contents for all to see. His hand passed over the secret compartment, sloshing through her undergarments with the gentleness of a newsboy pandering the latest scoop. Livy's breath seized. A dent in the compartment poked from behind the cloth at the corner of the hidden panel where she'd concealed her pistols, ammunition, and other items destined for her covert purposes. His fingers slid a mere inch from the spot.

"You are busy today, *non?*"

He stopped his search, perusing her body with his dark gaze as if seeing her afresh. She fisted her fingers but kept a steady grip on her expression, tilting her smile with more welcome.

He glanced down at her papers again. "We stay busy during this season, Mademoiselle Moreau. You come from the south?"

"*Oui.*"

His expression took a wary turn. "You are a long way from home."

"I am visiting my cousin in Combourgh."

His gaze shimmied down her again. "Who is this cousin of yours in Combourgh?"

"Camille Baudin."

His thin brows shot northward "The actress?"

Livy released a light laugh. "Well, she prefers to be known for her fashion designs, but it seems her occupation as an actress has garnered more attention."

The man closed her trunk and offered her papers but didn't immediately release them. "I will return your papers on one condition."

"Oui?"

"You introduce me to your cousin should ever we meet again?"

Livy unfurled her smile, tugging her papers free from his hold. "But of course. She always enjoys meeting charming men." She gripped her trunk and slipped her papers into her bag.

"And you are traveling alone, mademoiselle?"

"I'm afraid so." She hesitated. "My fiancé was looking forward to meeting my cousin as well, but I'm afraid his illness prevented his coming and I must, instead, travel alone."

"A beautiful woman should never travel alone."

She turned to the familiar voice. *Christopher!*

"You're here!" Without thought, she launched herself into his arms.

He stumbled from her embrace shocking her to her senses. She pulled away, her cheeks reddening at her own behavior, but he wrapped his arms around her in such a tender way she never wanted to leave. Something broke inside of her...or mended. Whichever it was, she held tighter to both the feeling and the man who inspired them.

He was alive. She pinched her eyes closed. *Thank you, thank you.*

His cheek moved to the side of her face so that his lips breathed near her ear as he'd done in the plane. "First crying and now this? I have a feeling I'm a bad influence on you, my dear Constance."

She narrowed her eyes at him but refused to move too far from his touch. "I'm inclined to agree." She avoided his eyes and dusted off the shoulders of his shirt. "What if you promise to stay safe and sound from now on so I won't have to resort to such demonstrative affections?"

He tipped her chin with his finger, capturing her gaze again. "I rather like your demonstrative affections."

Only after she gathered her paradoxical emotions and left the warmth of his arms did she notice what had escaped her attention during her moment of relief at the sight of him. His pallor had paled and a thin line of sweat beaded his brow.

"I'm happy to see you, darling." She sent a look in her periphery to the guard who watched their reunion with a little too much interest. "But I wished you'd stayed at home until you were fully recuperated."

"I must admit I was afraid I may lose your heart to one of these dashing men in uniform." His playful response sounded nonchalant, but the slight tension in his voice pierced her awareness. Her gaze traveled the length of him. He favored his right side, and the slightest shift of cloth at the waistline of his shirt bulged from added material. A wound?

She shot a grin to the officer who'd just finished with her bags. "I should think these men in uniform are sensible enough to rest when they've experienced an extended illness." And with ease, she slipped his arm into hers to add stability to his stance.

"Most men are fools to their hearts, are they not, monsieur?" Christopher directed the question to the German guard.

He grinned but did not reply, instead gesturing toward Christopher. "Your papers and bag, sir."

"Are you truly cross with me, darling?" Christopher's voice cradled the endearment and she smiled.

Livy locked her gaze with his. "I'm happy you are here, more than I have words to say."

HE KNEW SHE'D PLAY THE GAME LIKE AN EXPERT AND SO SHE DID. With ease, she stayed by his side, allowing him to appear much less in pain than he was. He only prayed the makeshift bandage held long enough to get them to a place where he could check the damage.

"I need to see to your wound with privacy, but there's at least one other person in our box," she whispered as they walked down the train corridor.

"Then let's pray the bandage holds for the two-hour trip."

She rolled that smoky gray gaze of hers then looked ahead. He could almost hear her mind working. Without warning, she opened a small door to their right and jerked him inside, securing the door behind her.

Within a half-second, Livy turned some switch and a dim glow illuminated the tiny closet. Electrical panels labeled with words such as lighting, heating, and cooling, lined each wall. An electrical closet? "How did you know about this?"

She tugged off his coat she still wore. "I studied the blueprints of the train before we left England."

"Of course, you did."

"Unbutton your shirt."

Her focus took on a new intensity that he dared not disobey. "It's really not as bad as it appears." He unbuttoned his button-down. "The bullet had a clean exit through the flesh. It's nothing serious."

"Do you have additional bandages?"

"Actually, you do." He nodded toward the coat in her hands. "There should be one medical kit sewn into each side of the lining."

By the time she'd retrieved the kit, his shirt hung open, and he'd tugged his undershirt up to reveal the bandages at his waist. A red stain was beginning to seep through his clumsy work.

"This isn't serious?" Her raised brow nettled him like a school marm's reprimand, but her fingers on his skin proved gentle, cool.

She peeled the cloth away, and he winced at the sting.

"It looks as though the bleeding has slowed considerably." She tugged off the rest of the bandage and stuffed the scraps into the pocket of his coat. "It must hurt but I'm glad you are otherwise unscathed."

Her bowed head brought her rosewater scent closer as she worked to replace the bandage. He grinned at her choice of perfume. Simple. Subtle. "You must have prayed very hard."

"I'm certain God's ears will be happy for the reprieve."

He lowered his forehead to the top of her head. "I'm happy you're safe."

She looked up, her face so close to his that he could make out the curve of her every eyelash. "And I'm happy you didn't disappear again. I don't care to lose another fiancé, especially the right one."

"The right one, is it?" His grin spread as her arms swept around his waist to secure the new bandage. "Took you long enough."

"Took me long enough?" She shot him an impotent glare. "I could have used a little more help from you in the matter. All this silent brooding doesn't do any good for me at all."

"Silent brooding?" He couldn't help it. His grin widened further. "I see you missed me."

"And I'd not care to miss you again, so I expect you to be on your most excellent behavior and survive the night, won't you?"

"I'll do my best," he whispered, pulling her attention to his face. "If you'll promise the same."

Before she could answer, the closet door rattled.

Livy's eyes enlarged, and she looked down at his half-wrapped wound and open shirt. Christopher did the only thing he knew to hide their covert dilemma. He turned his body so that hers blocked the door, jerked her against him to cover the bandages, and caught her sudden gasp with his lips.

Her mouth softened against his perusal. As Livy's body relaxed into his, her lips adjusted to the onslaught. Had she never been kissed before? The thought gentled his approach. He caressed the side of her face, her skin feather-light beneath his fingers, and she hummed some sweetly intoxicating little sound of delight as she slipped her arms around him. If she were pretending, she was doing an excellent job. He pushed another palm across her cheek and into her hair, coaxing her to tilt her head and enjoy the tender exploration of their lips.

Together was the right place to be.

A deep voice cleared from the doorway.

Christopher reluctantly pulled back from the long-awaited taste of Livy Rake's lips. He'd wondered what it would be like to kiss her, and reality exceeded his imagination. Livy stared up at him, her eyes almost glowing.

The poor steward stood in the doorway opening and closing his mouth like a codfish, his face turning new shades of red.

Christopher kept Livy against him and offered the steward a shrug. "She said yes."

"To what?"

"To my proposal." Christopher placed a kiss against her head. "We were searching for a little privacy to celebrate. This was the only place for such...intimate reveling, as you can imagine. Not so romantic but certainly private."

The disgruntled steward passed another look between them, and Christopher felt Livy's hands slip to his waist and begin fastening the buttons of his shirt without garnering any notice.

"Show me your tickets, and you can celebrate all you'd like. But I warn you, my supervisor will be through this compartment in no more than five minutes, and he will not take kindly to lovers in his electrical closet."

"Of course!" Christopher turned, as if to reach for his bag, completing the buttons of his shirt while Livy drew out her own tickets from her handbag.

The steward took both of their tickets. "Five minutes. And if you know what's good for you, less." He waved the tickets forward as he gave the slips of paper back, sending another wary glance at them before closing the door behind him.

Livy turned and stared at Christopher, her breathing shallow. She appeared even more fetching than usual with a rosy glow in her cheeks, as if her mussed hair weren't enough.

She drew a handkerchief from her bag and wiped his face. "I'm afraid you're wearing more lipstick now than I am."

"The reward was worth the cost."

Her movements stalled, and her gaze switched to his face, a humored grin tipping her kissable lips into a lovely smile. "It's a good color for you."

"I'd like to kiss you again, Constance. Without the audience." His grin twitched and his thumb traced her jawline, inspiring a tremulous breath from her lips. "And since we *are* engaged, it seems rather appropriate."

She pinched the lapel of his shirt, drawing him closer, requesting more from his heart than a kiss. "It's difficult to make plans in a world at war, Monsieur LaCroix."

He captured her gaze, forcing a hundred unspoken promises into his stare. "I almost lost you once from caution." One of his hands slid down her back, drawing her flush against him. "I'd rather make memories than regrets."

She'd always imagined she'd not enjoy kissing.

Two mouths pressed against each other in some sort of rhythmic dance? But the tenderness beneath the kiss, the caresses and care, somehow transformed her misinterpretation of lips on lips into something indefinably sweet.

His palm slid from her cheek to cradle the back of her neck, and his forward motion tipped her already crooked hat to the back of her head. His eyes, deep and layered with myriads sapphire hues, called for every ounce of her attention, bringing her closer. The noises of passengers outside the closet door droned to a murmur as Christopher snatched her lips and her breath in one sweeping touch.

Her lashes drooped and an intoxication of oakmoss draped her senses as his soft lips settled against hers. Her attention and almost obsessive focus inventoried each sense, each touch. Spiraling warmth. Deep breaths. Cool fingertips against warm cheeks.

He coaxed her heart to life in a beautiful newness flavored with surprising familiarity. Had she always loved him and never understood until now?

His kisses left a lovely trail of tingles in the wake of their caress, inspiring her reciprocity. Upon this second attempt, instead of standing in shocked stillness, she could abate her growing curiosity about this entire kissing experience. She slid her hand up his chest and over the intricate weaves of his shirt until her fingers reached the skin at his neck. His breath caught. His kiss deepened. Her hand gripped for more of him, slipping into the cool folds of his hair. Every sensation, taste, and smell exploded in colors in her mind as brilliant as any fireworks. How had she not known he cared for her?

She loved him. She smiled against his lips, the acknowledgement bringing such an alarming joy she barely contained a laugh. Everything from the past three years clicked into place. And he loved her in return, as odd and abrasive and nonconformist as she was.

He drew back, his breath in shaky retreat. "You're laughing at me at a time like this?"

"No, I'm just happy. It's a rather alarming realization."

He grinned, his eyes sparkling. "Your happiness?"

"Actually, wanting to marry my fiancé. It's a new experience for me."

Christopher placed a swift kiss against her mouth. "I have every intention of it becoming a fixed expectation." He released her, reached down for his jacket and bag, and drew her arm through his, leaning close. Tingles along her neck mirrored the level of his voice. "On and off the field."

CHAPTER 8

Danger lurked in the shadows and daylight in France, but fear clung to Christopher's thoughts for a very different reason. He'd given his heart to Livy once again, fallen into the gentle sway of a time-worn friendship and a rekindled love. When his mind needed emotionless clarity, her presence proved a lethal aphrodisiac.

One he longed to indulge in.

During the train ride to Combourgh she'd warmed his right side, the chink in her usual distance allowing him glimpses of the woman he once knew. In whispers, meant to be lovers' conversations to onlookers, they recapped the information they knew of Camille Baudin and reviewed what intel they had on the lost airmen.

Their usual banter slipped into the conversations, an easy step back into their friendship. Paired with the closet interlude, his thoughts unraveled too easily for the good of this mission. In London, at their homes, they could live the lives those kisses promised, but not now.

What had he started with a simple kiss? He shook his head. Who was he fooling? A kiss was never simple and neither was Olivia Rakes.

Christopher drew her hand into his, bringing her attention to him. "That kiss, Livy."

"*Those kisses.*"

"Yes. *Those* kisses."

"They can't happen again. Not in earnest." She shook her head, fisting her hand beneath his. "There is no room for distraction."

"An understatement to the extreme if you're referencing *those* kisses, my dear."

She graced him with a much too infrequent smile. "Indeed."

"But now it's time to play the game and keep our heads clear of our hearts." He rubbed a thumb against her knuckles. "We can store those pent-up feelings for later."

"Later?" Despite her placid expression, her fathomless gaze hesitated in his.

He squeezed her hand. "I will do everything in my power to keep you safe."

"I'm not worried about *my* safety."

"We both know what we're doing. We agreed to it in full knowledge of the possibilities."

"That was before I knew you...you loved me."

Her hesitant words confirmed the depth of her feelings. He raised her hand to his lips. "And I will love you still, but we must put it from our minds for now."

She arched her narrow brow, the faintest smile on her lips. "Once something enters my mind, Monsieur LaCroix, it is unlikely to leave, and this information is much more impressive than my usual fare." Her face sobered. "I *will not* lose another person I love."

She'd said it. Aloud. And the unintended admission nearly broke his resolve to not kiss her again. "What do you mean?"

"During my last mission, I let Clara die."

He pinched her hand in his hold, remembering the story his father had told him of Livy's undercover meeting. "That isn't true."

"If I'd been faster, deciphered the clues with more speed, we could have escaped together instead of her insisting on staying behind."

"We're all taking chances, Livy. We sign on knowing the risks and what this world may look like if we don't win."

She stared at their entwined hands and her brow crinkled. "I shouldn't have left her behind."

"Sometimes for the greater good, for the safety of the many, we have to leave someone behind." He squeezed her hand once more. "And in those moments, it's the right choice to make."

She refused to look at him.

"In our profession, we attempt to control everything. Our movements, our voices, our stratagem. Any thread within our power, we strive to keep in its place, but ultimately, we are not in control, and we must trust our choices and the kind hand of Providence with the outcome."

He touched her chin, turning her to face him, her unruly eyes marbled into gray-green. "Don't forget. Our mission is only part of a greater Hand at work. We are not alone in the field."

LIVY AND CHRISTOPHER BOUNCED IN THE BACKSEAT OF THE CAR AS they traveled along cobblestone streets to Mademoiselle Baudin's. Bombed buildings huddled next to storefronts housing limited wares while thin children clutched their mother's hands as they stopped for any amount of food left at vendors' stands. Subsequent air raids in other places had left Combourgh unscathed, but one look into the faces of French men and women on the streets told a truer story.

A world of oppression.

On the edge of the town, their car stopped in front of an ornate apartment building, a renovation of an older chateau, whose white façade faced the billowing countryside stretching into the late afternoon horizon. Christopher had endured many bases of operation, but he preferred the luxurious sort, if he had the option, and he was certain the British airmen would too.

"I've heard a great deal of stories about your cousin," Christopher said, using the knocker and giving the massive door a solid hit.

"If all I've read is true, we'll play the part of secondary characters to her immense personality, knowledge, and skill."

The door opened to reveal a young woman of service, her white apron and hat dressing her in an almost demure appeal, as only the French could do. "May I help you?"

Livy took the lead. "Good day. I am Constance Moreau and this is my fiancé, Adrien LaCroix. I believe my cousin is expecting us?"

"But of course." The maid bowed her head and opened the door for them. "Please, follow me."

A strong scent of citrus perfume cloaked the air and almost propelled Christopher to the front stoop, but, like the best trained operatives, his body betrayed nothing. Even when his eyes began to water, which blurred his vision from the pink décor almost luminescent in the sunlight filtering through the windows, he remained stoic.

"Well, well, it seems cousin Evelyn was not lying when she spoke of your beauty, my dear Constance."

A woman in a flurry of sheer cloth and dark satin emerged before them, her lips the same ruby hue as her exotic gown. This couldn't be the Resistance agent Adele, could it? The one known for helping tens of airman escape occupied France?

"Thank you, my dear cousin. I am overwhelmed by your generosity in welcoming us."

Livy's bright response proved her acting skills were intact. Christopher couldn't help but grin.

"And you are the lucky fellow, non?" Camille floated forward, taking Christopher's hands in her own and wrapping him in her perfume until his nose tingled. She examined him then squeezed his hands. "You have a good heart, I can tell. And are quite easy on the eyes." She turned to Livy. "I see you know how to choose a husband. Did you pull him from the line of soldiers, cousin, or from the law, for he's too roguish to be a man of the church?"

Livy's smile bloomed. Her gaze landed on him. "We are childhood friends."

"Ah, you caught him early. Very good. It is the best way to train a husband."

"And what would you know of husbands, mademoiselle?" Christopher sat in the chair she offered.

"One does not have to marry to know husbands." Her impish grin returned. "And I've known many."

Well, her reputation certainly matched all he'd heard of Agent Adele. Influential, adored, and wealthy, she used her wiles and connections to obtain more information in three months than his spies would in six. Having the cover of an actress and fashion designer certainly played in her favor.

"And this romance began as children?" She reclined onto the chaise, her gown fluttering around her in a cloud, casting a glance to the maid at the door. "How quaint."

Ah, she was setting the stage for her servant. Excellent.

Christopher tilted his attention to Livy, allowing his war-weary thoughts a moment's respite on happier times, finding the fun of sincerity in his game. "I don't know that I would call it romance at first. It started more as charity."

Livy laughed, and his heart stumbled in response. He loved her laugh.

"He had a notorious lisp when he was little, and the boys were horrid to bully him about it."

"So she took me on as her first subject, correcting my lisp with the tenacity that only the strictest schoolmarm could appreciate." She smiled at his description, her expression softening with an admiration he found fascinating.

"And he did the same in return, didn't you, dear Adrien? Taking on the nasty boys who teased my severe introversion."

"I intend to continue picking off bullies for you for the rest of our lives."

Livy's smile brimmed. "And I yours."

Camille looked between them, her lips slit into a curious grin. "A perfect match, I see. Well, we must get to work straight away." She turned to the maid. "Antoinette, leave us and make certain we are not disturbed." Camille's dark eyes glittered with mischief. "We have an engagement party to discuss, non, and from the looks of it, no time to waste?"

"Yes, miss." The servant bowed her head and disappeared through the doorway, snapping the door closed behind her.

"I do apologize for the extreme scent of perfume." She gestured with her cigarette toward Christopher. "Your nose is red from the effort not to sneeze, Monsieur LeCroix. I gave my servants the day off yesterday so that I could house munitions here for pickup from the

Resistance. The smell of hay and powder was too obvious, so I cloaked it as only the most eccentric of ladies can do." She took a draw from her cigarette and sighed. "There are benefits to playing the part of a dramatic woman, you see?"

"Your reputation precedes you, mademoiselle," Christopher added, finding the notorious Agent Adele everything he'd anticipated and more. She'd survived an entire year as a spy in the most treacherous of areas. She had to be very good at her job. "In the most excellent and extravagant of ways."

She blew out a stream of smoke and smiled, examining him with acute observation honed in their mutual craft. "I am pleased to know it." Her attention shifted to Livy. "I had not expected the two of you to be such excellent actors. Especially you, Constance. You are new to the field, I understand." Her grin crooked when she returned her focus to Christopher. "But I have heard of you, Adrien. The Stoic, if reputations can be trusted."

He smiled at the nickname. "I can play my part, mademoiselle."

"Indeed. I actually believed the two of you are in love." Camille laughed for a moment, but her dark gaze studied them as if she knew the truth.

Christopher brushed away her concern. "A part to play, of course."

Her grin tipped a little wider. "Of course." Her gaze swept between them once more, and then she sat up, her nonchalant demeanor falling from her expression like a cloak. "We do not have much time. I've heard that your five airmen have been captured and taken under the watch of General Wolfe and his associate, Lieutenant Bauer." Her red lips slanted into a sneer. "A particularly vile sort of man." She rolled her eyes. "And a horrible kisser."

Christopher exchanged a look with Livy. He readjusted his assumptions and took inventory of the agent shining through the actress's guise. "What do you know so far?"

"He's imprisoned the men in the basement of a country house outside Combourgh, but my sources have not been able to locate which house. I've narrowed it to six, in particular, to suit such an arrogant man, but we haven't time to investigate all of them. We must learn the location before he transports our airmen to Germany...or worse, dispatches them."

"I assume you know how we can obtain this information?" Livy asked, leaning forward, eyes lit with readiness.

"I have places in the vicinity where the lieutenant frequents. You will take one of them and I the other. Our goal is to collect intel as to the airmen's location and then..."

"We'll sort out a rescue plan," Christopher finished, holding Livy's gaze.

"If we can locate them." Camille's lined brow rose in challenge. "I have a plan, of course."

"A plan? To gain intel?" Livy watched Camille's movements with a mixture of awe and scrutiny. Christopher imagined she was trying to sort out a way to emulate some of the behavior for her own role. Either that or she was completely bewildered by the dramatic antics of their contact.

"It's a little risky." Camille tilted her head and clicked her tongue. "But the best plans usually are. And though our German men are shrewd, they are still men and susceptible to certain inducements." Camille sauntered toward Christopher, the look in her eyes giving him fair warning of her intentions. "How are you at the art of...distraction, Monsieur LeCroix?" She pulled Christopher up by his jacket and pressed her body against his. Her palm took a slow, alluring slide up his chest to his shoulder. Christopher almost grinned, knowing the skill well and thankful for his training against the womanly wiles.

"And by distraction, you mean..." Livy cleared her throat, but to her credit, her expression remained neutral. "The art of seduction?"

Camille turned to Livy. "Seduction is a powerful tool in any spy's inventory, but for a woman it is particularly useful." She ran a palm down Christopher's cheek, taking his chin into her hands and drawing him almost to a kiss. Livy flinched in his periphery. Well, perhaps this practice in distraction would prove a little fun.

"It creates distraction, and in response, loosens their tongues, which is what you need to glean information from our nasty German neighbors, particularly in their usual haunts." She lowered her lips to graze Christopher's chin. "You will muddle his thinking, divide his mind and his passions so that he will concede information without even knowing it. Much wine and strategically placed touches create opportunities for our men to find their way safely home. It is a clever little game to play and not altogether unpleasant, if the prize is right."

Christopher looked down at her, his grin spreading, immune to the typical yet perfectly executed ploys. She pushed him into the chair with a groan. "You are no fun. I didn't get so much as a hooded look or quick intake of breath from you. Which proves you are either very well trained"—her gaze slipped to Livy— "or your heart is contentedly captured already, non?"

"Perhaps a combination of the two?"

"Ah, you are not so stoic." She laughed and nodded her approval before relaxing into her chair and taking up her cigarette. "A clever defense, *mon ami*. But I think your fiancée is inexperienced in the ways of romance, non?" Her attention shifted to Livy. "She is a good girl who needs a little training in the art of the game?"

"She's a quick study," Christopher offered, a little uncomfortable with any lessons Camille Baudin might choose to teach Livy. "I am certain she is equal to the task."

"I can learn anything you need to teach me. And fast," Livy added, her chin raised for the challenge. "My memory and gift of imitation are my strengths."

"Is that so?" Camille blew out another stream of smoke, one ebony brow raised. "Perfect. You have the shape and dark look to those curious eyes of yours." She nodded, examining Livy through another long silence. "Yes, you will do. I shall prepare her tonight, and we will enact our plans tomorrow evening."

"Tomorrow evening?"

"Oui. To gain intel. I know where we must go and what must be done." Her red lips wrapped around the end of her cigarette, poised in a smile before she released a stream of smoke. "But I do not think you will like the plan."

CHAPTER 9

Livy refused to adjust the tightly fitting gown as she turned the alley corner. The bordello, an unassuming building simply framed in white, housed one of the most notorious brothels of the city. Camille had warned her to dress "like a lady" because even though the *maisons closes* were filled with every possible kind of intimate pleasure, the law under Nazi occupation encouraged an indecorous disguise. The clientele, though, liked their women stylish.

The gown cinched Livy's waist much like she imagined corsets knotted around her grandmamma before the Great War. Despite the snugness in some areas of the frock, other pieces hung loose, exposing her shoulders and neck in an alluring contrast to everything she preferred. Of course, the gaudy red of the fabric drew as much attention to her body as like the stain drew men's eyes to on her lips.

Camille had spent the previous evening coaching her. Christopher provided input, though from his continual grimace he appeared nearly sick with the task. Not too different from the way Livy felt as Camille modeled those seductive movements on Christopher. But as Camille described them and guided her, Livy's mind opened to more understanding of the nonverbal interactions of the sexes…and the temptations.

And she couldn't wipe the memory of Christopher's expression when she'd emerged in her crimson gown for the evening. To have responded without so much as a flinch to Camille's overt caresses, his eyes lit with a dark interest, a drawing, to her. He found her attractive.

She walked with a little more confidence in the direction of the bordello, the knowledge of Christopher's feelings a tantalizing discovery in this sweet romance of theirs. What woman wouldn't wish the man she loved to gaze at her with such unfettered passion? Perhaps enjoying the womanhood God had given her wasn't such a horrible lot after all.

The lights from the brothel shone against the sky, bringing with them a raucous noise and the thick scent of liquor. Of all the choices of missions, *this* was her lot. No, she didn't like it at all, but time wasn't on their side. They had to use the means within their grasp to gather information as quickly as possible. Any hour could be the airmen's last.

When she found Charlie, she'd ensure he heard of the massive sacrifices of comfort she had to make on his behalf.

And she *would* find him.

With a deep breath and a palm to her chest to ensure the pen pistol remained hidden securely in a most intimate spot, she crossed the street to the brick building. La Belle Vue touted to the world that it was a respectable inn, but from the garish sneer on the doorman's face, Livy knew the truth.

A whitewashed tomb.

Oh God, help me walk into the mouth of hell and return whole.

"What a beautiful vision that has emerged from the shadows this evening. Do not remain out of reach, *liebling*."

Ah, a German doorman. Most likely on guard. He took her hand and pressed a lingering kiss to the inside of her wrist. Her senses screamed to the alert, but Livy fisted them into the coolness of control, unhinging the actress within.

She smiled, running her fan down his cheek. "I thought all of the handsome gentleman were on the inside of the inn, not waiting in the dark streets, unnoticed and alone."

His grin widened, and he tugged her into his body, wrapping his fleshy arm around her waist. "If you want to stay outside, I will pay you full price without the middle man." His hot mouth settled at her ear. "A good price for a good time. Madame Blanc need never know."

She pushed away with a laugh, her stomach roiling from the man's grimy breath. "But I am here on reference from Monsieur LaPonte for the lieutenant. A gift, so to speak." She took a forged letter from her pocket. "I should not wish to disappoint him with my tardiness."

The man's face paled. He dropped his hold on her and glanced at the paper. Monsieur LaPonte's reputation for ruthless business, and even more violent actions to his enemies, carried a poignant influence. Lucky for her.

"Another time, perhaps? For the...um...good price, as you say?"

The man's grin resurrected as he opened the door for her, lingering much closer than necessary. Myriad sounds and scents assaulted Livy's senses as she stepped into the garish entry that contradicted the building's outer simplicity. Grecian columns cornered a room in which an orchestra of bow-tie-donned men provided lively music as if in one of the most lavish London restaurants.

She'd read her fair share about the bordellos, a home-away-from-home for the warmongering Germans. Livy frowned, her heart twisting, as well-dressed ladies led uniformed men up an elegant stairway and out of sight. She would never condone the purpose of brothels. Whether to provide a lucrative income, make ends meet, or find pleasure in temporary satisfaction, the behavior all ended in the same vanity. Yet, after seeing the forlorn faces of the French people in the town, how many widows entered this building to provide food for their tables? Desperation and lust upturned lives. Oh, the depth of the cost of war. Casualties much deeper than bodies that changed lives forever.

God, rescue these people!

A few rooms opened on either side of the entry, showing elegantly furnished gathering places as innocent as any sitting room at home. Handsome and distinguished soldiers, likely SS based on their black uniforms, relaxed in settees while conversing with one another or finely dressed women who wore gowns as exquisite as seen in any theatre. Champagne and other beverages of choice bubbled in endless supply along with laughter and benign caresses. To the naked eye, the entire scene appeared as harmless and simple as an overindulgent house party.

Her reflection peered at her from a gilded mirror to her right—at least, she thought it was her own reflection. The application of additional cosmetics and a well-placed blond wig had transformed Livy's appearance into someone wholly different. A sultry, sophisticated woman no one would recognize. Tonight, she wasn't Olivia Rakes, the old-maid linguist, or even Constance Moreau, the starry-eyed fiancée, but Angelique, a sultry, sophisticated 'gift' who knew how to play the game and wasn't afraid to charm important information out of powerful German soldiers.

She looked ahead at two sets of massive double doors near the back of the entry hall. With a tilt of her head and a bit of drama infused by Camille's tutelage, Livy slid off her fur coat.

A man caught her fur and placed it over his arm, his bright blue eyes taking her in from her bare shoulders down the length of silky concoction of burgundy satin. "I was wondering when you'd get comfortable, mademoiselle." He spoke in impeccable French, but German influence colored his vowels. Clean-cut lines strengthened the look of his face. Handsome, most certainly. Mid-forties. A soldier. She examined him with greater scrutiny. No, an officer, if she had a guess. Time to play the game.

"This is my first visit to the illustrious La Belle Vue, and I am overwhelmed by the detailed elegance."

His attention took another detour down her body before he slipped her arm through his. "And are you visiting with a specific purpose in mind?"

She raised a brow to him, adding a crooked smile for humor. "Education." She looked toward the closed double doors. "And pleasure."

She took another look around the room. Christopher was supposed to meet her here.

"Then you've found the right place. I would be happy to provide you with both. A mutual partnership, perhaps?"

She prolonged her gaze on him, as if studying his appearance, and then smiled. "I have been sent here as a particular...gift for a certain Lieutenant Bauer." She touched a palm to the man's smooth face. "But should he prove absent, I would entertain this idea of a...partnership with you."

"Lieutenant Bauer is a lucky man tonight." The officer nodded and steered her toward the double doors. "He has not yet arrived but should appear very soon. I will escort you to his table."

A woman garbed in golden chiffon met them at the doors. "Ah, Captain Bruce, who have you brought with you to my place?"

Madam Bergeron, the mistress of La Belle Vue. The grand woman fit Camille's description to perfection.

"Madam." Livy gave a slight bow to her head.

The woman studied Livy with eyes that missed nothing. "You know me, but I am unfamiliar with you, mademoiselle."

Livy retrieved her letter and offered it to Madam Bergeron. "I am here as a special guest to Lieutenant Bauer, madam, from your faithful servant and patron, Monsieur LaPonte."

The woman's eyes sparkled and she examined Livy afresh, all reserve stripped from her expression. "Ah, Gerard has found a new girl, has he?" Madam Bergeron walked closer, touching Livy's face with a cool, crinkled palm. "Untouched. A country girl? The lieutenant's favorite."

"Untouched and curious, madam."

"Curious enough to work hard for your family's bread, I should think?"

"I would do whatever necessary for those I love, madam." A heartfelt truth within Livy's disguise.

Madam Bergeron patted Livy's cheek, her gaze softening with... understanding, perhaps? Sadness? "The lieutenant is good to his girls, especially his new ones. You will find him a generous patron and most patient tutor." She tipped Livy's chin with the pad of her finger. "And he shall not take too much from you on the first acquaintance, ma chère. He is patient."

Livy swallowed the bile rising in her throat and covered it with a timid turn of her gaze. Thank the good Lord for His protection, even in this. Mercifully and strategically for Livy, Camille had been correct in her assessment of both Bauer and Madam Bergeron. "That is a comfort on both counts, madam."

"Captain, show the lovely mademoiselle to the dining room. The lieutenant should be here shortly."

The doors opened to a dimly lit hall lined with clothed tables. A balcony framed the room where onlookers, usually in pairs or threes, looked down to those dining below. Half-clad women walked the room, some serving drinks and other sitting on men's laps in a most intimate fashion. Here lay the truth behind the entry hall's elegance. The real debauchery within the walls.

How fast could Livy attain her information and escape?

"The lieutenant's table is there, the one with the yellow roses in the center. He is particularly fond of yellow roses. His wife's favorite."

Livy's smile stilled on her face. A tribute to his wife as the lieutenant enjoyed other women? Unthinkable.

"Thank you, captain. You've been most helpful."

"And I'll remember your offer, should the lieutenant disappoint you." He kissed her hand and exited the room.

The scent of expensive perfume and wine spoke to the quality of patrons in this establishment. A few of the men near the door sent heated looks her way before the women in their laps snagged their attention with even hotter kisses. Livy straightened her shoulders, keeping the goal in mind. Intel. Charlie. She *had* to do this.

"I think I've been looking for you my whole life." The familiar bass voice rumbled behind her, and her neck tingled in welcome response.

She turned and smiled. Christopher had never looked more appealing. An open collar and disheveled dusty hair added to his overall appeal as a rescuer in this motley combination of ruffians.

"Your whole life, sir? I certainly hope you've brought a life's worth of wages with you in due recompense."

His grin crooked, ruthless and pleased all at once, and her heart swelled with a desperate and deep love for him. Could God send Christopher to rescue and calm her even in the middle of this horrible place? Her breath caught as he slid his palm around her waist and pulled her onto his lap. Goodness, if his cerulean gaze alone ignited an anticipatory sizzle beneath the skin of her lips, what would his kiss do?

She cradled his head. "I'm beginning to believe you are notoriously late."

His chuckle near her ear inspired a cascade of tingles down her neck. "I just want you to miss me."

"Ah, so it is more self-serving than absentminded."

His gaze found hers, the dear friend emerging behind the façade of a brothel-attending rake. "I'm rarely absentminded." She rolled her eyes at his boyish charm, a trait becoming more and more endearing with each passing hour. "But I did notice your excellent connections from the start. Passing the inspection of both Madame Bergeron *and* Captain Bruce. Brilliant, darling."

Darling took on a sweeter lilt, settling deep within her like a promise.

"Aren't you the least bit distracted by the...displays in the room?"

"The eyes may distract but the mind keeps us constant and the heart keeps us faithful."

She slid closer to him, rubbing her palm up his chest to his neck, keeping up appearances. "Are you a poet now?"

"Actually, that is a quote of my father's."

"Your father?"

"He's a secret romantic but don't let on that you know."

She looked at him then—past his debonair appearance for tonight's excursion, past the charm that transcended Christopher into Adrien LeCroix—considering his father's words in the context of their maddening situation. In the middle of the horror of war, of the desperation and corruption of La Belle Vue, her mind came to startlingly sweet revelation. Even in this horrid place, Christopher's embrace enveloped her in an intangible understanding of coming home. A feeling she'd never experienced anywhere except in those still, small moments where faith came to life in her heart. She'd never fit anywhere else. Except now. In this strange, duplicitous, dangerous world. With him.

For one suspended second, they were Christopher and Livy in a world of pretend.

He held her gaze, his expression softening into a look that touched her heart. His palm warmed her cheek, and drew her close. "I'll keep you near until the lieutenant arrives, which should discourage other, less well-intentioned blokes from approaching you."

"Won't you get into trouble?"

His eyes glowed. "It is my first visit here. I can plead ignorance, if I must."

She chuckled as he pulled her into a strategic embrace that gave her visual access. "Now," he whispered, hoarse and deep as he trailed kisses to her ear. "What do you see with that perceptive magic of yours?"

She swallowed, her cheeks and every fabric of her skin aflame as she pulled her foggy thoughts away from the feel of his breath on her neck and warm hands against her. Without further enticing distractions, he held her, unmoving, giving her mind freedom to clear. Seconds passed as Livy took inventory of their surroundings, adding a careless touch to Christopher's head or kiss to his lips as she changed position to observe each face, each location.

"I haven't seen the general or lieutenant yet, but Captain Krause is here. This may be easier than we thought," she whispered into his hair. "Even though the captain is with his regular lover."

"How on earth can you tell she is his regular lover?"

"It's obvious," Livy replied, running a palm down his face and to his neck, keeping up appearances. "She has touched him fifteen times in the last two minutes, all familiar caresses more than the heated sorts. Like this." Her palm moved across his chest and back to his cheek, coaxing him closer. "Their kisses are more lingering than passionate, another sign of familiarity and deeper interests than mere lust. You see?"

He grinned like an utter idiot into her face. Her fingers filtered from his golden locks down to his ear and gave it a little pinch. "We need to focus, *mon cheri*, despite the alluring distractions."

"I see Mademoiselle Baudin's tutorial was most effective." His whisper carried a promise to which her body responded.

"I'm a fast learner, as you well know."

"Indeed, I do hope you'll keep up the practice in our future, more private, encounters, *cherie*." He cleared his throat and moved his lips to her ear. "I will attempt to coax the lieutenant for information, once I suss out a way to separate the two lovers."

Livy glanced at the pair. Perfect. "I don't think you will have to.

They are arguing. This is good for us. And the general just arrived. He is looking around the room. For me, I would wager. The doorman likely shared the news of my arrival. You should leave me alone before you get into trouble tainting his virginal prize."

A pure look of disgust crossed Christopher's face before he cloaked it. "I don't like this idea."

She ignored him. "Go after the captain's lady. He hasn't had enough to drink to loosen his lips but she may prove most helpful."

He pulled away, searching her face. "The lady?"

Livy peered over Christopher's shoulder. The woman slapped the captain's face with such force that he stumbled. "Most certainly. It is my understanding that nothing unhinges a woman's tongue quite as well as wine and scorn."

Christopher took her face in his hands and held her gaze. "Be careful."

"And you." She playfully pushed him away and sashayed toward the commanding presence of Lieutenant Bauer.

She swallowed to wet her throat and fixed her attention on her mission. At least a foot taller than her, he smelled of bourbon and cigars, but his eyes lit with awareness at her approach.

"You must be my *cadeau* from Monsieur LaPonte." He spoke fragmented French, which might have been due more to his alcohol consumption than his linguistic prowess. Could the war have turned in a sour direction for the Germans today?

All the better for Livy.

"Oui, monsieur. I am Angelique."

"Angel, yes. A perfect name for a perfect gift." He slurred in some form of half-German, half-French. "I shall sample your delights in my favorite room tonight."

Livy forced her smile and distracted his roving hands with another drink, slipping the faintest drop of liquid into the glass. Only half reached the bourbon as the liquid sloshed on the table. Would the drug still work? He fussed over her, touching her arms, her back. Whispering drunken endearments into her hair. Attempting to 'soften her' for the activities ahead, she gathered. She stifled a cringe.

The drug would unhinge his thoughts just before it incapacitated him, and before he expected any favors, she hoped, or else she'd resort to her pistol, a choice she didn't want to make.

Laughter peeled into her playacting, so she sneaked a peek in Christopher's direction. He had the lieutenant's lady cradled in an intimate hold, whispering something into her ear. A ridiculous smile graced her face, and as she laughed, she ran her hands down his back to rest a bit too low on his hips.

The Stoic, my eye! He appeared to enjoy himself a little too much at this playacting.

Livy switched her attention to her drunken diversion, pinching her curiosity closed. Christopher was doing his job.

"Let us find a more secluded setting," the lieutenant murmured, pulling her to stand along with him. "I plan to enjoy my last night of freedom in the arms of an angel. Monsieur LaPonte's enticing bauble is sure to help me forget this gray day for my people."

Livy stifled her immediate reaction to recoil from the man's hand as it pressed in at her waist. Aha, the Germans had experienced a loss. His emotions would prove even closer to the brink, she hoped. "My poor dear, you are a busy man and must carry such a burden."

"Too much work, if you ask me. Caretaking, instead of taking the field. If they'd had me today..." His words blurred into a growl.

Livy patted his cheek, sharp with stubble. "You are too important for such work?"

He tugged her toward the stairs. "Ya. Keeping walking dead men alive, but not for long."

Livy took one last look behind her. Christopher was still clutched in the woman's arms. She drew in a deep breath and slid her palm over the lieutenant's back as they mounted the stairs. "You shall be free of the walking dead men?" She laughed. "You are already tired of the French?"

"Not French," He mumbled in his stumble, jerking her into him before righting himself. "You smell like spring." His mouth fell hard against hers, hot and heavy. "Ah, you taste like spring as well."

Livy trailed her fingers over the man's face, turning his lips to her cheek instead of her mouth. "Better than the dead men you babysit, non? Are they nasty British?"

Bauer laughed and reached for the handle of the nearest door in the hallway. "Stupid British. They think they can fly over Germany's France without getting caught. Imbeciles."

Livy's pulse leapt into motion. He knew where her brother was! She danced her fingers up the buttons of his shirt then slid her palm around his neck. "You are too smart for them, mon cher. However do you manage tending to such idiots?"

His sneer materialized. "I have no need to hide." He beat a fist against his chest. "This is Germany's France."

He pulled her into the room and attempted to close the door, but Livy stuck her heel in the gap just before the door snapped shut, leaving her shoe as a clue to her whereabouts for Christopher.

Bauer slid off his jacket, followed by his suspenders. "Come closer. I plan to remedy your problem of being overdressed."

Bide time, Livy. She tugged her hand free from his hold and reached into her hair to loosen a pin. "Patience is a virtue, non? Sit back and I will give you a show."

He groaned his pleasure and settled into the lush red high-back by the bed. His glassy eyes took on a fiery glint but no added clarity. He wouldn't remain conscious for long, with or without her intervention. She released another pin and moved in a dancing motion, swaying like the pendulum of a clock. Methodical. Hypnotic. The motion caused an almost dreamy effect on her sloshed victim.

"I hear you are most generous and patient. A man of importance, non?" At the sixth pin, the remainder of her hair loosed.

"Importance."

"I am sorry you must feel so underappreciated in your work. And this is your only means to relax, *mon petit*? No sweethearts?" She placed her bait. "No grand parties?"

He captured her waist and drew her to him. "Wolfe will give his grand party, will laugh in the face of Britain, and I will relax then. Celebrate German victories and British defeats."

A grand party. Camille had mentioned a house party in a neighboring chateau. The location?

With more force and clarity than she'd imagined possible, the lieutenant seized her mouth with his own. His hands gripped her waist and moved downward, tugging at her gown as he went.

She pushed at his massive chest, praying for the drug to take hold, but he gripped her so tightly that her hands were pinned between them. Ideas whirred through her head, each attempt meeting a rejection in his stalwart pursuit. Cool air wafted against her bare back as he released two more buttons of her gown. "Give me a kiss, Angel."

He caught her by the neck, drawing her forward, tightening her ability to breathe.

His mouth lowered against hers. She bit his lip. He howled and pinched her throat harder, cutting off her scream. She struggled, mentally counting the seconds before she lost consciousness, praying for relief.

Shadows fogged her vision. She clutched at his hand to no avail.

Then, as if from heaven, a strategy Agent Atkins taught her flew to the forefront of Livy's mind. With what strength she could, she dropped her full weight to the ground and swept her leg beneath his, knocking him off balance. When he stumbled to his knees, she jumped onto his back, holding to his throat with an iron grip. His arms swung to knock her off, but she held tightly to him, his movement disconnected and inaccurate from the combination of drug and drink. He attempted to throw her off, but she clung to him until he collapsed onto the ground. She waited a few more seconds to secure his unconsciousness then pushed off his back and rolled him over. He breathed.

With quick movements she slipped his slacks from his body just as Christopher entered the room. "Your timing was impeccable."

"Not exactly." He knelt in front of her and took her face into his hands, examining her with a furrowed brow. He growled before tugging the fabric of her gown up over her bare shoulder. "Forgive my tardiness."

"You do have a reputation." She swallowed through her pained throat and offered a wobbly grin. The grimy touch of the lieutenant's hands still waved across her skin, but she held Christopher's gaze, absorbing the tenderness like a balm, a gentle healing against the memory of her encounter with Bauer. "I am fine."

His smile softened and his palm lingered against her cheek. "Yes, you are, and strong. Don't forget."

"Help me get him into the bed. With any luck, he'll not remember what happened."

Christopher took the top half of the massive man while Livy grabbed the lieutenant's legs. "I see you were too much for him."

She smiled, a needed and natural reaction to Christopher's humor after the uncertainty of the last few minutes. "I already have my sights set."

His attention dropped to her neck, no doubt seeing some of the after-effects of the captain's brusque behavior. "I'm glad to hear it."

They placed the captain on the bed and covered him as if he'd been asleep. With one last glance around the room to ensure nothing looked out of place, Livy nodded, ready for the next course of action. "I have information to help us locate the airmen."

"Excellent. Me too."

"Let's go rescue Charlie."

CHAPTER 10

Christopher stood on the balcony of Camille's apartment, staring into the morning sun as it swelled on the horizon. Light bathed the world in a pure glow, a promise of a new day. For two years he'd worked with the Resistance, putting his life at risk, watching his fellow comrades die, but nothing prepared him for the utter helplessness of rescuing Livy in the brothel.

He'd charmed the captain's lady into giving information of the country house in which the captain stayed. He delayed his exit to ensure he'd retrieved every piece of intel he needed, but in doing so, Livy had been hurt.

He closed his eyes. Thank God worse hadn't happened.

How could he lead her into the viper's nest in another chance he might lose her forever?

She'd proven her abilities. Even after the first three small assignments before leaving England, she'd maintained magnificent composure, but he'd wondered how she'd fare in the harder places. In the life and death situations.

She was brilliant.

He opened his eyes, staring at the whispers of morning hues, begging God for another day, another opportunity. Praying for Livy's safety no matter the cost for him. Everything had changed. He offered a reluctant grin to the heavens. Yet somehow, everything also had stayed the same.

Was it possible to have both worlds in one? It seemed too much to consider...too much to ask.

"It wasn't your fault, you know."

Livy's voice soothed him as she stepped to his right, facing the dawn, her hands poised beside his at the railing. "You told me on the train that we serve a higher purpose than our feelings and our agendas. Do you believe it?"

With a begrudging groan, he nodded, knowing the direction of her conversation. "Yes."

"I am as committed as you to this cause." She faced him. "And I...I don't want to lose you either. Not ever again."

She took his hand in both of hers. "But I understand now that I can't be afraid of failure at every turn. We are trained for this mission, called to it. Together. And we must see it to the end."

"And bring Charlie home."

She nodded with a small smile. "And bring Charlie home."

With a hint of uncertainty, she stepped toward him, into his arms, and rested her head against his shoulder. She fit so well against his heart, in his life. He rested his cheek against her hair, pressing the scent to memory. Even after the lurid surroundings of the night before, she held to an innocence he hoped these circumstances wouldn't taint.

Christopher brushed a hand over her hair. "Are you alright after last night?"

"I am." She looked toward the horizon then to him. "You were there."

"I would have been there soon—"

"No." She shook her head. "I don't mean during the horrible incident. After. In the car back to Camille's house. When you...held me." Her brow puckered. "It's the closest to any other person I've ever felt. You are...dear to me."

He pulled her hand up to his lips, unable to find words.

"I think I've always had some connection to you, even since childhood, but I never knew what to do with it. How to understand it. What to call it." Her gaze flitted to his. "Until now."

He slipped a finger beneath her chin and tipped her face so he could read those changeable eyes. "And what would you call it?"

Her smile tilted up ever so slightly as she leaned closer, a glimmer in her gray eyes. "You're the spy. You sort it out."

Christopher caught her smile with his lips, lingering long enough to let her know he understood. He pulled away, tracing her bottom lip with his thumb.

"I know failure," she whispered. "You know I do, but you've taught me that we are part of a grander mission, bigger than ourselves. I'm proud to be a part of this, even with its shadows and scars."

His fingers found her neck and smoothed a touch over the bruise he knew remained from Lieutenant Bauer's attack. "Tonight will either prove a success or..." He cleared his throat and held her tighter to his side. "From the layout of the house, in Camille's estimation, we could walk directly into a trap."

She looked up at him, her gaze clear, certain. "Then I'll leave this world as a proud product of my profession, a faithful servant of my country, and...and a grateful recipient of a good man's constancy."

He kissed her smile and gave her chin a playful chuff. "I think with the two of us and the daring Agent Adele, we have an excellent chance to outwit the Hun."

"Especially Agent Adele."

"I will give them a night they'll never forget." Camille's voice sounded from the room behind them. "With style, of course."

∞

"What if we're in the wrong place?" Livy asked as the chauffeur drove their car over the country road. "I know that the intel we collected points to this chateau, but we're not absolutely certain."

Dressed in a high-necked silvery gown from Camille, Livy felt like a famous actress from a moving picture. Camille had even had the maid style Livy's long hair into some fashionable twist pinned by a silvery barrette at the base of her neck. Somehow, most likely due to Camille's celebrity status, she'd secured invitations to General Wolfe's house party.

"Then we shall enjoy a fine party, exquisite wine, and leave respectably early." Camille tossed a grin from the seat facing Livy and Christopher in the limousine. "This is the place." Camille waved her gloved hand in the air. "Between the information you gathered, Adrien, that the captain visited his lover at a place in the east of the city, we could narrow the estates down to two possibilities. Constance's confession from Captain Bauer confirmed the presence of British airmen." She nodded. "Yes, I feel quite confident in our choice."

Despite the closed chauffer's barrier window, Camille lowered her voice and leaned forward, her golden gown sparkling in the fading sunlight outside. "We will stop at Café Fleur long enough to secure the other agents and their positions in our plans. Three are to assist us."

"Leon and Gabriel must be two of them." Christopher matched her volume. "I trained Leon. Who is the third?"

Camille's dark eyes sparkled. "Daniel, the dangerous, our saboteur. I absolutely adore him. He reminds me of my father. Brilliant, with a knack for mischief, though he has much more hair than my father ever possessed." She waved a hand to them. "He also complimented my designs and criticized my acting. I fell in love on the spot. Who could not want a man who has tastes in designs and lights fires." She sent a saucy grin to them as the car came to a stop in front of the café. "Tonight, we will leave quite the impression."

THE MANOR HOUSE INVITED THEM FORWARD WITH FESTIVE LIGHTS and a false sense of welcome. Christopher scanned the building, counting six guards at the door and on the periphery. He turned to Livy. "What do you see?"

Livy kept her face toward the window. "Nine...no, ten guards so far. You may have missed the two on the roof and two snipers on the second story. The blacked-out windows in the front of the house give a marked clue, of course."

Her saucy grin teased him. "Now you're just showing off."

"You are very useful, aren't you?" Camille laughed, pulling her gloves tight against her wrist, covering the tiny pistol attached to the inside rim of her left one. "With your quick mind, Constance, you would be perfect in the research division." She looked at Christopher. "She's worth keeping 'round, non?"

"That is my heartfelt intention, mademoiselle."

"Clever man. I should have kept my Louis 'round for much longer, but the Fritz decided to steal him from me much too soon." The flair in her eyes dimmed for a moment, highlighting her loss. "But I am ready to introduce a few of the Boche to my new pistol, Genevieve. Small, but…um…rather effective."

Christopher's smile twisted into a grimace. It was a good thing that Mademoiselle Baudin was on their side. He looked at Livy just before a footman stepped to open the door. "Let the game begin."

LIVY'S FAMILY BOASTED MIDDLE-CLASS ELEGANCE, BUT SHE'D NEVER experienced anything like this. The entry hall swelled with immaculate statues looking down at arriving guests from their perches. Christopher stayed close, playing his part as the lovestruck fiancé, which suited him well, to Livy's way of thinking.

Camille wooed the crowd with her natural charisma, drawing the German officers into easy conversation and admiration. Her popularity as a film star eased suspicions quicker than expected. Livy kept her smile at the ready, taking cues from the mistress of distraction in her gown of gold.

"You are the illustrious Camille Baudin, of which I have heard many great things." A broad, commanding man greeted them as they entered the ballroom, his stance stalwart, his expression striking. The scent of ink and oil provided an undercurrent aroma to his staunch cologne, his very presence demanding attention.

Livy tempered her snarl. *Wolfe.*

The general's gaze riveted on each of them, finally pausing on Camille as she took the lead. "I was pleased to receive your invitation, General. You have quite the reputation yourself."

Wolfe's tense face relaxed, softening the hard edges into a more approachable man.

"We have every desire to keep life as it is in your beautiful country, mademoiselle. The movies, the food, and, of course"—he waved a hand to the ballroom— "the romantic and exquisite atmosphere."

"You are certainly succeeding." Camille turned toward Livy and Christopher. "Which is why I was pleased to bring my cousin and her fiancé with me. They are from the country, and I hoped to show them how well you treat your French neighbors. May I present Constance Moreau and Adrien LaCroix." Wolfe basked in the admiration, Camille's charm working like a spell.

"Indeed." Wolfe's gaze slid over Livy with renewed interest. "Just because we occupy this country does not mean we cannot appreciate its many treasures."

Camille's smile gave nothing away. "But of course." She glanced at Livy. "Constance was nervous to attend. She has only heard the nasty rumors of soldiers stealing food and livestock from families in the country."

The general offered his hand, the movement pinching the fabric at his chest. A hidden pistol. But the weapon didn't peek as much concern as the exacting way he examined each one of them. He took in details like Livy did. Methodically. Making judgments and winkling out truths.

Despite the urge to look away, Livy returned his stare, smiling.

"I hope you will take this experience to your people in the country, Mademoiselle Moreau. Show them we are here to celebrate the beauties and arts of France, not destroy them."

Livy took his offered hand. "It has proven a pleasant experience so far. Adrien was particularly impressed with your sculptures."

Wolfe took Christopher's hand. "Indeed."

"They appear quite old. Perhaps Grecian?"

"You enjoy the arts, monsieur? Yes, they are Grecian. And we have some fine paintings in the gallery. A Van Gogh and several Renoir as well as many others." Wolfe's eyes lit. "You see, life and love and art go on in France as they should. Our presence has not changed this place." He turned to Livy. "And now, you must dance." He gestured toward the ballroom. "Monsieur LaCroix, do not be too vexed if your fiancée is stolen away. The men outnumber the women two to one."

And from the look of things, most of the men held the posture of soldiers rather than aristocrats.

"May I have the pleasure of the first dance with Mademoiselle Moreau?" Wolfe offered his hand and looked to Camille. "With you as my next partner, Mademoiselle Baudin?"

"*Mais oui.*" Camille offered a coy smile. "I shall look forward to it."

And with a coquettish smile over her shoulder in perfect acting fashion, Livy slipped away from Christopher and into the arms of the enemy. There was no turning back now.

CHAPTER 11

Christopher drew Camille onto the dancefloor. "I see at least eight guards in civilian garb."

"With a distinct concentration of them by the west hallway." She smiled, belying their topic of conversation to the onlookers. "From the hand-drawn blueprints Daniel provided, I believe that direction leads to the kitchens."

"And the cellar."

"Oui. A perfect place for prisoners."

Livy laughed and drew Christopher's gaze. He loved her laugh, even a superficial one.

"Do you see the server with the tray of wine by the hallway?"

Christopher spun Camille around to get a better view. A dark-haired man in his black-and-whites waited with a tray in hand. "Yes."

"That is Daniel, our saboteur. He changed his hair color for our mission tonight." She grimaced. "It does nothing for his complexion at all. He has such lovely auburn hair." Her sigh ended in another plastic smile. "I will communicate our plans to him. I can only imagine what little surprises he's created for our host."

Christopher grazed the man with a glance, careful not to keep attention for too long, but the chap held a strategic location near the guarded hallway. Excellent to have someone on the inside to give them such valuable information. "And I'll speak with Constance about the plan."

They spent the next half hour mingling with the guests, all the while taking inventory of the location. General Wolfe found a way to confiscate Livy for another dance, which was an excellent opportunity for her to garner more trust and information, but the possessive hold the man kept on her left little to be desired.

As the dance drew to a close, Christopher stepped forward and slid Livy away with an effortless turn.

"Reluctant to part with your liebling, Monsieur LaCroix?" The general's moustache twitched with a challenging grin.

"*Certainement*, General, to such an engaging man as yourself. I have scarcely heard her laugh as much in the past few months as she has while dancing with you. Humor is a certain path to the heart, non?"

Wolfe chuckled. "Tell this to my previous wife."

"I would question her tastes in humor and men, General," Livy added, sending Christopher an almost-scathing frown. "One can never be too certain of another's character and loyalties, can they?"

Wolfe's brow hitched, his expression melting into an apology Christopher didn't fully understand. "I do hope your tongue is as skilled as your fiancée's, monsieur, for I believe you have a great deal of explaining to do."

Wolfe caught Camille's hand as she passed, drawing her into his arms to the sway of the music. "If Mademoiselle Baudin finds me equally amusing as Mademoiselle Moreau, I may entertain the idea of another party before the month is out."

The pair glided away and Christopher drew Livy close, his face against hers. "I don't like that man."

Her body remained stiff, but her smile pressed against his cheek. "Jealous, mon petit?"

"Most fiancés should be if they know what is best for their hearts."

She drew back, her brow puckered with a...pout? "Did you notice the west hall?"

Her clever turn of topic proved he'd hit the mark of her emotions.

Ah, he was beginning to enjoy this tenderness more each moment. "Yes, Camille and I will attempt to make our way behind the guards."

She tipped her head and searched his face with those mesmerizing eyes. "Then I suppose I must offer up my distraction, non?"

"For other people besides me, you mean?" Her lips tempted him nearer. "I'm guessing by your unwelcome body language that you have something unpleasant in mind?"

"You're not going to like it." She inventoried the room. He could almost see the thoughts spinning through her mind. "Do you see the captain there? Captain Weber is his name, from what I understand. A lonely sort. His wife left him only a few months ago."

Christopher followed the gesture of her chin to a tall man standing on the periphery of the room. Livy smiled at the man, the expression almost coy. Camille's lessons were working.

His stomach pinched. Perhaps espionage wasn't the best choice for Livy, or perhaps Livy in espionage wasn't the best choice for him. "I have a bad feeling about this."

She shook her head, rehearsed tears welling in her eyes as she looked up at him. "We must make this work, and you are taking the more dangerous route, I fear."

He cupped her shoulders, their dance ceasing in the middle of the floor. "Your allegiance is not to me, Camille, or even your brother." She tilted her head, studying him, and his throat tightened around the words. "We have come to fulfill a duty. If the time comes when you must choose, keep a steady head and heart with that knowledge. *Tu comprends?*"

She raised a challenging brow. "Perhaps my head and my heart are strong enough to hold them all without fail."

He shook his head. "But mine is not. Promise me, for *my* sake, that you will keep to the plan, no matter what happens."

Her gaze faltered but he tipped her chin up until she looked at him. "Promise me."

"For your sake?" Her lips firmed. "I promise."

With those words, she pushed him away and smacked him on the cheek. "How dare you deny it, over and over, Adrien. Captain Krause saw you. Why would he lie to me? Have you been playacting all along? What...what am I to you?"

Christopher blinked from the impact then caught on to the charade. "Come now, my dear, let's continue this conversation elsewhere. We wouldn't wish to ruin the general's fine evening."

"You've already ruined this evening for me. Why...why would you feel the need to visit La Belle Vue?"

A woman gasped. A man covered his wince with a hand to his lips.

Christopher raised both palms, approaching her slowly as she backed away, his voice a coaxing whisper. "Come now, darling, we are not married yet."

"Not married yet?"

He dodged another swing from her.

"I can't even look at you right now." She buried her face into a handkerchief. "Leave me alone."

He glanced around the room and beckoned for her to draw closer, the ploy working marvelously. "Constance."

She pushed past him on a direct course for the powder room then tossed a glare over her shoulder. "I...I don't even know you, Monsieur LeCroix, and nor do I wish to."

"Adrien! You imbecile." Camille rushed after her, the plan in perfect time. "How could you do this to her?"

Christopher rubbed his jaw and stifled a grin. Perhaps Livy Rakes was made for espionage after all. One thing he knew for certain—she was made for him, scowl and all.

LIVY RUSHED THROUGH THE CROWD, USING HER HANDKERCHIEF TO pat her eyes. One glance behind her revealed Captain Weber's sharp attention on her. Their brief conversations this evening set the stage. He was interested, and she needed to exploit that interest.

His suit lay lax against his body, a good sign that he might be a rule-bender. She teased a glance over her shoulder, and his brow tilted along with the slow rise of one corner of his mouth. Perfect. Now if she could only seduce a man who still had his wits about him.

The door to the powder room caught before Livy closed it, and Camille entered, latching it behind her. She scanned the small room. "Quite the dramatic exit, ma chère."

"Step one, non?"

Camille's scarlet lips tipped. "You were made for this, you know. I see it in your eyes. It feeds you. Do not forget."

Warmth spilled through Livy, confirming Camille's assessment. Despite the danger, or perhaps because of it, every facet of her mind surged with energy, clarity, and purpose. She felt alive, ready for the challenge, righting wrongs.

Camille stood beside her at the mirror, pinching her cheeks to deepen their color. "Daniel has uncovered where we must investigate. It is up to us to..." She wiggled her brows. "Distract then disappear, so I trust you will do as I've taught you?"

Livy stared at her own reflection and took a deep breath. "I will certainly try." She drew her lipstick from her purse, but Camille paused her hand.

"No, no, cousin. I have a much better choice for you." Camille brought a tube of lipstick from her purse and place it in Livy's palm. "It's one of the newest creations, sure to leave a lasting impression."

Goodnight Kiss marked the golden tube in a curly script. Livy's eyes shot to Camille, who smiled in her pleased way. Livy had only just heard of lipstick laced with a drug to render the man kissed unconscious. A small plastic strip accompanied the vile to protect Livy's lips from the effects.

"Make the kiss count. A light touch doesn't give the lasting effect any man should wish for in a kiss. Leave him in no doubt of your intentions, oui?"

"Oui." Livy's grin tipped at Camille's subtle hint, and she pushed the tube into her handbag before touching up her cosmetics.

Livy followed Camille toward the powder room door, but just before leaving, she reached down to give her right heel a firm twist. It loosened with the tiniest crack but didn't completely detach. Careful to keep a lighter step on the right foot, she reentered the ballroom behind Camille.

"My heel is unsteady, Camille. I think it caught in a tile of the floor when I ran from the room a few moments ago." Her voice rose enough for onlookers to hear. "I do hope it will hold for the evening."

"Your heel?" Camille glanced down at the shoes, a frown puckering. "They are certainly not a pair of *my* shoes." She clicked her tongue. "My dear Constance, you should know better."

Her eyes sparkled with the mutual understanding of the scene ahead. She placed a comforting arm to Livy's arm. "Are you certain you wish to join the party again after such a shock?"

Several gazes focused on them as they stood on the precipice of the room, their conversation drawing the desired attention.

"I will not allow my delinquent fiancé to ruin my evening." She added a tremor to her voice for effect and stood taller, sending a lingering glance in Captain Weber's direction. "In fact, I may take every opportunity to find my own pleasure in it."

She followed Camille into the room, as a man immediately snatched the spymistress for a dance. Christopher stood by the entry hall, one of the footman delivering his coat to him as if Christopher were leaving the party.

Livy took a glass of wine from Daniel's full tray, meeting his eyes with only the slightest connection before glaring at Christopher. Once he returned the look, she shifted away, pinching her eyes closed as if the very sight of him stung. With a little stumble, from the obvious emotion of her distress, she pressed down on her right heel, breaking the shoe then exaggerating her fall into Daniel. His tray crashed to the floor, shattering a half-dozen glasses and their contents onto the marble floor while she made certain as much of the contents of her wine glass landed on her gown before it slipped from her hand.

She crumbled into a heap, widening her eyes at the apparent disaster as onlookers stared her way. In tandem, Christopher slid around the corner of the hallway, blocked from the guests' sights by positioning and Daniel's adjustment.

So far, so good.

"Mademoiselle, are you all right?" Captain Weber offered his hand, and she leaned into him with a tremor.

"I...I'm so...sorry."

"Constance, what on earth happened?"

Livy worked up her watery vision and found Camille's face. "My... my heel." She looked down at her broken shoe and pinched her eyes closed to release the tears. "Forgive me." Her gaze scanned the stained floor and splattered glass. "Do forgive me, General. What a clumsy fool I am! I've ruined your party."

General Wolfe came to her side, examining the damage and offering her as consolatory an expression as she supposed he ever gave. "No harm done. A distant memory in no time, liebling." He gestured for Daniel and another servant. "Clean up this mess and bring more wine." He shifted to the small stringed orchestra in the recesses of the room. "Play."

The bow-tied men responded with a lively piece.

"Your gown, darling. It's ruined." Camille's voice filtered through the commotion.

Livy stared down at the dark stains soaking through the silver. "We should go. Look at me."

"You were distracted, *ma petite*. Heartbroken." Camille took her handkerchief and attempted to blot the stains. "Where is Adrien? If I get my hands on him, I'll ensure he never marrie—"

"He's already left the house. I saw him retrieve his coat and go without as much as a by-or-leave. That shows you the depth of his affections." Livy shook her head, tears resurrecting with more fervor. "I was nothing to him." With a sob, she buried her face into her handkerchief.

"Coward. He'd best hope we never meet again," Camille growled.

Servants swept in, clearing the scene as onlookers returned to dancing.

"I will send for the car." Camille frowned, taking in the disaster then bestowing her most pleading expression on the general. "I cannot apologize enough for this mishap. And on such a lovely night. We will go."

"There is no reason to leave on account of her cretin fiancé." His stance relaxed, and he took Livy's hand, drawing her attention to him. "See here, there is no reason to leave. In a few moments all will be as if it never occurred." Wolfe waved his hands to his servants at work. Daniel had conveniently disappeared from the tuxedo-donned men.

"But, monsieur, my dear cousin cannot continue in her current state." Camille gestured to Livy's soiled gown and broken shoe. "We *must* go."

Wolfe measured the situation as if he stood on the battlefield. "I will not have you or your cousin leave in such a way. *Nein*. We are well equipped here." He spun to Captain Weber. "Escort Mademoiselle Moreau to the Edelweiss Room. She will find a suitable substitute for her current gown, I should think." His dark gaze fastened on Livy, intimidating, waiting. "Will that meet your approval, mademoiselle?"

"My good sir, I cannot thank you enough."

He fingered the sleeves of her gown. "I suggest you choose the blue one, like twilight. It would suit you better than this."

Livy shed a few more tears, took the general's hands in both of hers, and kissed them. "*Merci*, cher general. Merci."

"No young woman as lovely as you should leave embarrassed. We shall remedy it." He placed Livy's hand into the captain's. "Make certain she receives special care, Weber. I would have her smile again tonight."

"Of course, sir." Captain Weber's sea-green eyes swept the length of Livy, pausing on her broken shoe. Without another hesitation, he slipped his arms beneath her and lifted her off the ground, taking determined steps up the stairs.

Livy barely had time to catch her breath, let alone prepare for her next move.

"I am here to assist you, mademoiselle." A dour maid appeared at their side.

"I shall see to her," Weber answered, cutting the woman a dismissive look.

The maid shrunk away, and Livy drew in courage for the next task —stealing Captain Weber's keys and, hopefully, harmlessly dispatching him.

He moved effortlessly down the hallway but for the slight limp in his right leg. A war wound? His dark hair brushed back from his impressive forehead with an almost inconsequential wave, and he lowered her onto the floor and in front of a door with the ease of someone younger than the limp would have him look.

"Thank you for your kindness, Captain." Livy lowered her gaze but allowed her palm to glide a slow retreat over his shoulders before she wobbled a step back from him. "Is this the room?"

"Yes," he answered, pulling a set of keys from his pocket. "Follow me."

"The general locks all of his bedrooms?"

The shadow of a grin lit his face. "Only for special rooms. His daughter stays here when she visits." Weber opened the door and allowed his gaze to trail down Livy once again. "And she is close to your shape."

Livy slid past into the elegant room of cream and pale green. "The closet is here." He gestured to a door on the other side of the room.

"You are well acquainted with this room?" Livy teased, and his smile broadened.

"The general's daughter is not the only lovely lady I've escorted to this place."

"You're a rogue then, Captain?"

Weber stepped to the closet and rifled through the items, choosing a shimmering blue ankle-length gown with a silver lining like stardust that would leave the wearer with one shoulder bare and one covered. It was exquisite.

"Will you wait outside to escort me back?"

He crossed his arms over his chest and raised a brow. "I will wait here. There is a dressing room." He tilted his head toward the door beside the closet.

Livy dabbed at her eyes again then offered him a shy smile. "Very well."

Within five minutes she'd slid into the silky garment and loosed her hair. She applied the plastic film to her mouth then coated her lips in the rich red lip color. With a steadying breath and a prayer for help, she reentered the bedroom where the captain stood, his position unchanged. When he saw her, his gaze turned dark, intense.

Every impulse within her urged her to turn and lock herself in the dressing room, but her mission burned a deeper groove of purpose. *Charlie. Christopher. The Resistance.*

"Adrien never liked me wearing blue." She lowered her gaze,

fingering the shiny material. "And certainly not something this"—she ran a palm down her side— "tight."

"Your fiancé is a fool," came the captain's gruff reply. He'd closed in, merely a few feet away. "So was mine. Ruthless. Unfeeling."

Livy's heart flinched the slightest bit. She would be ruthless to him too. How many British men had he killed? "I'm sorry, dear Captain. I'm learning that entanglements of the heart are quite dangerous and... and painful."

He slid another step forward, his eyes focused on her lips. "Ah, but my dear, the heart does not always have to be involved."

"No?" She swallowed, her throat growing dry at the part she must play. "I may prefer your sort of game then."

"I can teach you. You won't regret it. You will forget your idiot fiancé." His grin twitched and he brought his palm to her cheek, gliding its warmth down her neck. "The general charged me with making you laugh again. I take my orders seriously." He dipped his head and took her mouth in a long, thick kiss.

She gasped, pushing through the motions of her art, and finally broke away, breathless. "I...I don't think I've ever been kissed quite so thoroughly."

His palms moved down the side of her gown. "I have much more in mind for you, liebling. You will not remain sad."

Livy leaned forward, holding to his jacket as if her legs had grown unsteady. "How does one manage much more of such a kiss?" She breathed close to his mouth. "Teach me."

He wrapped his arms around her, pulling her to him for another kiss, then another, finally stumbling with her to the monstrous bed.

She attempted to distract him from the effects of the drug by gliding her hands up his chest and pushing his jacket from his shoulders. "I am suddenly warm, monsieur."

He looked up at her, dazed. "The wine and your kiss have me intoxicated."

Livy touched his cheek as his head dropped against a pillow. "Is that part of the game?"

"The best game." His words slurred. and he tugged her toward him until she fell against his body for another series of kisses, each growing weaker.

Within a few seconds his hands dropped to the bed and Livy pushed herself up. His chest rose up and down through deep breaths in sleep. She sighed then pilfered for the keys in his pocket. Seizing a new pair of shoes, she took her old left shoe and flipped a button on the inside, releasing the heel to reveal a hidden pistol. Left for lethal. She stuffed the keys down the—the only secure spot on her person— then walked toward the door, pausing to look at the sleeping officer.

"I'm sorry, Captain. I don't like to play games." Livy scanned the hallway before moving in the direction away from the ballroom. According to Daniel's sketched blueprints, a back staircase led to the kitchens. She froze as she rounded the next corner. A guard stood at the top of the stairs. He stared down the stairway in the opposite route of her approach. Livy plucked a beautiful floral teapot from a display on her right and raised it to strike, but the name on the bottom paused her assault. Chodziez? Her shoulders dropped. What a waste to destroy a work of art! She replaced the teapot with a modern ceramic vase.

Just as the officer turned, she hit him against the head. He poised, his lovely caramel-colored eyes wide, and then collapsed onto the carpet.

"Stop."

Another guard, pistol drawn, approached her. Livy reached for her pistol as a quiet shot sounded. She braced for the impact of the bullet but instead watched as the guard grabbed for his chest, eyes wide, and dropped to a heap in the floor, revealing Camille behind him, pistol up.

"Camille?"

She marched forward, stopping to give Livy a full-body glance. "I came to comfort you." She slit a saucy grin. "Lovely gown and the general was right. Excellent color."

Livy grinned and gestured to the guards. "I think we should put them out of sight. The bedrooms, perhaps?"

"Yes." Camille nodded. "And take their guns. Our airmen may need to help us fight our way to freedom."

CHAPTER 12

Christopher's search down the labyrinth-like hallways of the back of the chateau finally brought him to the base of a set of stairs that seemed to meet a dead end. He didn't have time for dead ends.

One doorway led into an enclosed garden, another to a hall leading to the kitchens, and the third to a closet that only housed a large trunk. Nothing else.

"I've set one explosive by the stairs. It's timed for half an hour," Daniel said. "It won't take long for the ladies' absence to be noted by the gentlemen, you know."

Christopher nodded and slammed his fist against the chest. "Our boys are here. I know it."

"But where and how do we get to them?"

Christopher stepped out of the closet and looked over the walls for the fifth time. Based on the sketches and his search, the most logical place for a stairwell was here. Was there a secret door? A hidden room?

He walked to the switch and flipped off the lights, taking another look through the room. He turned them on. Nothing. He flipped the off again, searching for any light seeping from unexpected places. Any gaps.

As he walked to the closet, the faintest glow, barely evident, shone from the crease where the trunk met the floor.

"I found something," he whispered. "Turn on the lights."

Daniel complied and Christopher took another look around the closet. Then he saw it—the shadow in the curve of the wall landed in such a way to give him a clue. The closet was recently built. A certain sign of a hidden spot.

"Someone's coming." Daniel lifted his pistol and backed against the wall.

Christopher did the same, taking the other side of the doorway. The quiet clip of sound paused Christopher's movements. Sharp, not dull like boots. Heels.

He raised a palm to stop Daniel's attack, and Camille slid into view, pistol to the ready.

"Camille." Christopher's harsh whisper perked her grin. "You're alive. I am suddenly optimistic."

Livy rounded the doorway and Christopher's breath stalled. Her hair fell with the fluidity of her twilight blue gown, a shimmering mix of magic and beauty. His throat closed around a response.

Camille tapped his arm with the side of her pistol. "I think you convinced her to keep the gown without muttering a single word, but now it's time to keep your head, Adrien."

"Of course." His gaze lingered in Livy's, silently assessing her status. Her faint smile was all he needed for clarification.

"What do we know?" Camille scanned the room.

Christopher explained his new discovery and all eyes fell to the chest.

"I have some keys." Livy turned her back to them and reached into her gown.

Christopher wrestled his mind away from her distracting behavior and took the keys she offered. On the third one, the key turned, opening the trunk and revealing a staircase leading down into faint gray-blue light.

"Do you have your torches?" Daniel placed a leg into the chest without hesitation.

Camille hit his shoulder. "And exactly where would we hide them in these?" She gestured toward her silky evening gown, her stare a skewer.

Daniel's dark brow jutted high. "You're able to hide a pistol in your shoe and keys in your..." He waved toward Livy.

"Oui." Camille shrugged a naked shoulder. "You have a point."

"Take mine." Christopher offered his to Livy but didn't release it until her gaze met his. He wanted to tell her she looked stunning. That her eyes danced like stars. But with an audience, such words didn't seem the best choice. "Be careful."

She appeared to catch the undercurrent of his meaning because the hint of a smile graced her lips. "You too."

Brighter lights flickered to life against the floor, guiding them, as they climbed down the stairs. The hairs on the back of his neck stood on end at the damp air. This staircase wasn't on the blueprints. They had no idea where they were going or what they might find.

At the base of the stairs the hall split in two directions, one leading toward other doors while the other kept its former cellar look.

"If prisoners are here, this is where they will be." Daniel gestured toward the darker side of the hall. "Military plans will be this way."

"And trouble," Christopher added. "I'll go with Daniel to set the explosives."

"We'll look for prisoners," Livy said, nodding before turning down the hall.

He watched her retreating frame until the shadows consumed her, saying a quick prayer for her safety before following Daniel down the other corridor. The lights continued to flicker, suggesting hasty installation for this makeshift headquarters.

Daniel stopped long enough to attach another explosive at the juncture of the secret staircase and their hallway while Christopher kept watch, and then they continued toward the sound of muffled voices.

German.

Daniel peered through the first door and held up three fingers then motioned Christopher to continue down the hall.

Christopher nodded, ducked passed the door, and continued down the hallway. The next room held two officers with backs turned to the door, both bent over papers on a table. A few quiet shots rang from the next room followed by a scuffle then silence. The men looked up and walked. One drew his pistol.

When the door opened, Christopher pulled the first Fritz out by his pistol and turned the man around to face the other just as the pistol went off. The other officer dropped to the floor and Christopher tightened his hold on the other man's neck until he lost consciousness.

In seconds, he'd taken photos of the plans, hid the men's bodies out of sight of the door, and met Daniel in the hall. This was a simple temporary German headquarters, and it appeared most of the guards had been assigned upstairs for the party instead of down below.

"I have one more." Daniel stood, dusting off his hands after setting another explosive.

"Good. Set it so we can catch up to the ladies."

A noise sounded from ahead followed by a crash of footsteps. Five guards led by General Wolfe rounded the corner. Christopher backed into the doorway of the nearest room, drawing Daniel with him. The only way out was past those men. From the sneer on the general's face, he knew he'd trapped them.

"I had hoped my suspicions were wrong, Monsieur LaCroix, especially about your ladies." He shook his head in patronizing disappointment. "It is a shame such talented people will not make it back home. Alive."

THE CELLAR OFFERED LITTLE LIGHT AND LESS HOPE, THOUGH THERE was plenty of evidence that the Fritz had renovated parts of the earthen walls for their specific purposes. A cloth used as a possible cot and a tin cup remained in one of the barbaric rooms. Two others held rows of wine racks and one more had the body of a British airman, dead for at least a day. He was from the same division as Charlie.

Livy's stomach squeezed with a wave of nausea. *No!*

How long had it been since the Germans removed the airmen? An hour? A day?

Livy squeezed back the burn of tears and moved to the next door, a smaller one. Camille worked a key into the lock. A rustle stirred from inside, and Livy readied her pistol. On the fifth key, the door unlocked and screeched open. An overwhelming stench wafted toward them, sending Camille backward and nearly tickling Livy's cough.

The torch light glared into the shadows, landing on two pale faces. Hollow eyes and gaunt cheeks spoke of their malnutrition, but their soiled uniforms branded them as Allies.

"We're here to rescue you." Livy entered the cell, helping one of the men to his feet.

"You? You...are ladies?"

"Ah, I see your airmen are also clever," Camille said in French, holding open the door.

Livy ignored her as the two men stumbled into the dim light of the hall. "Is there a Charlie Rakes among you?"

"Charlie?" One pilot placed his hand against the doorway to stabilize his steps. "He came in with us, but we've not seen him in two days."

Livy ignored the growing ache in her chest and steadied the soldier she was assisting against the wall. "I must check the rest of the rooms."

Camille nodded. "Quickly. We have less than fifteen minutes."

The next room revealed empty space and broken wine bottles, but when her key rattled the last door, a moan rumbled from inside. A last hope? "Bring the torch."

Camille moved to her side and shone the light into the small room. "We've come to get you boys out of here."

Two faces blinked at the invasion.

"Livy?"

Livy froze for the slightest second as realization poured through her, and then she rushed forward, taking the familiar face between her palms. His cheeks were thin and cold, his hair matted with dirt, but it was Charlie. "You're alive."

"What are you doing here?"

She took his arm and wrapped it around her shoulders, drawing him toward the door. "I've no time to explain. We must get you out of here."

A rush of unwelcome noise echoed down the hall. Voices. A

gunshot. An explosion shook the floor.

Camille met Livy's stare. "We've been discovered."

Heat left Livy's body. "Is there another way out?"

Camille shook her head. "We have no understanding of the cellars."

Livy searched the faces of the four men, her heart beating a fast rhythm against her chest. Young men, all of them. Were they to die now? After they'd gotten this far?

"No, no." Charlie shook his head as if clearing his thoughts. "We… we were brought directly here. Through a tunnel of some sorts."

"Yes," Another pilot added. He rubbed his forehead. "A secret door, back that way. We never entered the house."

The way they'd come? Livy and Camille followed the men as Charlie rubbed a palm against the wall. "I saw one of the Fritz pull a lever a few days ago. The wall opened."

Perhaps her brother had been in captivity too long. These dirt walls couldn't possibly hold a hidden door. But as the torch's light glistened along the earthen passageway, Livy noticed an unnatural indention in the cave. A doorway of wood the same color as the dirt, tunneled into the wall to make it more difficult to see.

"Here it is." Charlie's voice spliced the darkness.

The lever clicked and the wall gave way to reveal a metal door.

"The keys, Constance," Camille ordered, hand opened. "Now."

Gunshots blasted through the hallway. Camille drew a pistol from between her breasts and gave it to one of the soldiers then slipped up the cloth of her skirt and unstrapped another from her leg strap. "I assume you know how to handle these, gentlemen."

Charlie grabbed the other pistol. "Definitely."

A group of soldiers rounded the end of the hall and began firing in their direction. Livy shuffled through each key. One, two, three.

One of the pilots cried out, hit in the shoulder. Camille snatched his pistol and gave it to another pilot who wasn't wounded. Six, Seven. The key clicked into place and the door opened, ushering fresh air into the dank space. From behind the soldiers in the corridor another set of gunfire opened. Christopher rounded the corner, supporting a wounded Daniel.

"They're almost here," Livy called to Camille as they ushered an airman into the escape tunnel. "We can save them."

"Non." Camille shook her head. "Your orders are to get the pilots out." A bullet whizzed past, bouncing off the wall near them. "The mission, first."

Livy ushered two airmen through and turned to her brother, who was assisting his wounded comrade to his feet. As she pushed him into the passage, she looked back down the hallway. The Fritz outnumbered them three to one.

"Ah!" Camille grabbed her chest and dropped against the wall, pain wreaking havoc on her body.

"Camille." Livy knelt nearer. The dim light from the hallway revealed a dark stain spreading across her friend's pale gown.

No.

Camille grabbed Livy's arm, pinching hard. "Get them out of here."

"I can help you."

Camille shook her head, breath shallow. "No, you cannot. Too deep."

"I can try."

"There is no time." Camille's fingers dug into Livy's skin. "Don't waste my life. Save *them*."

Livy searched the space, desperate for another option, but her gaze found Christopher's down the hallway. For one second all the chaos slowed. The noise dimmed and they stood alone in the dark. His expression told all.

I love you. I'm sorry. Goodbye.

She shook her head.

He nodded in defiance, a final signal. With one last look, he aimed his pistol at a spot on the floor at the juncture of the secret staircase and hallway and fired. An explosion followed, directly in the Fritz's path, breaking their gunfire and sending most of them to the floor. Livy froze. *No!* He'd given his life to help her escape. In that second of smoke and rubble and complete agony, Camille rallied to stand, pressing one palm into her spreading wound and gripping her pistol with the other. "Run!"

She shoved Livy through the tunnel. "Now." With one last look, Camille charged into the hallway. "For France."

CHAPTER 13

Livy hid away in her usual spot in the music room, careful to stay free of as many onlookers as possible. The last thing she wanted, after the gravity of the last month, was to engage in frivolous conversation, playing the happy part she didn't feel. Her mother's fierce plea for attendance to Charlie's welcome home party finally broke Livy's self-imposed sequestration of silent mourning.

Alone, where no one could know the truth of her grief. An unanswerable consequence to an occupation born of secrets.

Even Charlie didn't know the extent of Livy's involvement nor was he at liberty to speak of it. Some day they might discuss her part in his liberation, but not now when memories still carried an oakmoss scent. She had no one except God to tell of her loss, and she'd burdened His ears with a healthy dose of both heart-wrenching questions and broken cries since returning home two weeks ago. The sound of gay music grated on her conscience, belying every ache in her wounded heart and boasting a joy she didn't embrace.

Except when she thought of Charlie.

The first week after she'd returned home, she'd believed Christopher somehow lived through the mission, and she anticipated hopeful news from Captain Dawson any day, but as one week stretched into two with no information, her heart sank with the sickening reality.

Christopher was gone.

She fought another bout of tears, biding her time until she could return to the haven of her room for welcome solitude. The letter in her hand presented a dilemma. An invitation to continue work with the OSE. Of course, the letter never mentioned the OSE but with usual military sleuth disguised the position as a research opportunity in linguistics. The small nuances and vague assumptions gave the intention away though. She'd been offered another chance, another opportunity.

Laughter rang from the next room, and Livy leaned around the corner to peek at the festivities. Her brother stood next to her father, and though Charlie's face still reflected the wear and abuse of imprisonment, he would recover. He shot a wink in her direction, his grin deepening the camaraderie of their shared secret.

A sense of gratitude poured over her gaping grief. He and the other three pilots would live, and somehow, despite her many peculiarities and failures, she'd helped bring them home.

She released a sigh, accepting her place in this bloody war. If her God-given gifts brought one more man home to his family, perhaps the heartbreak proved worthy of the reward.

For Camille. For Christopher.

She folded the letter and placed it into the pocket of her gown, making her choice. Life provided a patchwork of successes and failures woven together by love, faith, and the hope of something greater than this painful moment. For now, she knew her path for the near future and would walk it alone.

A shadow fell over her, blocking the light from the other room. *No, no, no! She had specifically told her father to leave any possible suitors on the other side of the wall.*

She stifled a groan and looked up.

"I know. I'm notoriously late."

Her breath caught. She blinked. *Christopher?*

Livy stumbled to a stand and gripped the chair for support, unable to move her gaze from his. She blinked again. Was this real? Her breath shivered on a single word. "How?"

His gaze roamed her face, but he maintained his arm's-length distance. "The explosion cleared a path, killing, or at least incapacitating, the guards until Daniel and I could get through, and then Camille..." His voice trailed off and he lowered before her to his knees. "She charged in like a bullet, shooting at the guards until she collapsed, making the path for us to reach the tunnel. One of the agents on watch saw us surface from the house as he was leaving the scene and hid us in the boot of the car, but even then. we had to hide out in a farmhouse without means to communicate with anyone. Daniel and I were both too wounded to travel. I had no way to send a message to you or my father without possibly giving away our location. Every avenue to return was blocked until only a few days ago, so we had to wait it out—"

"Prepare yourself—" Words she longed to say caught in her throat, but Livy forced herself to keep going, to show him just how much she loved him. "—Mr. Dawson. For I am inclined to be quite demonstrative in my affections." She propelled from her chair into his arms, pulling him as close as possible, breathing in the realness of him. Her palms roved over his shoulders, his back, ensuring that he wasn't a ghost to haunt her waking hours as he did her sleep. She buried her face into his neck, drinking in the oakmoss scent, the warmth and life.

He was alive.

Thank God.

His warm breath moved over her hair as he held her. No declarations. No kiss. Just a rush of gratitude too great for words. She laughed into his shoulder as tears streamed over her cheeks. Crying and Christopher, it seemed, somehow went hand in hand. She sighed, drawing him closer. She'd keep both.

There was no knowing how long they stood there, clinging to one another and this second life they'd been given, but Christopher drew away first, brushing a hand over her damp cheek as he removed his handkerchief to wipe her tears.

"I must say, my dear Livy." His grin crooked, gentle. "I have a soft spot for your demonstrative affections. I think you ought to display them more liberally as a rule."

She cupped his face between her hands, staring into his eyes, memorizing his face and this moment. "I believe I've finally found the proper inspiration for them. Tears and all."

He kissed her head. "You know, surprisingly there are a few married couples who work together in our particular occupation." His gaze probed hers, one brow raised in unvoiced question. "Or we could quit. I would…for us."

She pressed a palm to the lapel of his jacket. The shadows under his eyes marked days with little sleep and recovery from loss of blood. She'd felt the bandages beneath his shirt as they'd embraced, tender on his right shoulder. But this was their life, their choice.

"Christopher Dawson, I am certain I am better with you than apart from you, wherever that may be."

His grin widened, and he leaned close. "Then Fritz beware, and God steady my heart." His voice lowered to a whisper. "Because I mean to marry a spy."

And she meant to kiss one, which she proceeded to do for a very long time.

ACKNOWLEDGMENTS

As with any story-creation, there are many people with me at the helm, keeping me on track, praying for me, and sending encouragement. I'm certain I'll not mention them all, but here are a few:

Thank you, *Marisa Deshaies* for your amazing work on the edits of this story, your patience with my time-constraints, and your encouragement. Someday, I'll write a Mr. Darcy.

Roseanna White, I am amazed by you! Thank you for sharing an ounce of your creativity in pairing with me to make this amazing cover. It suits the story of Christopher and Livy perfectly.

I cannot imagine celebrating any of my stories without my amazing *Street Team*. You ladies are remarkable, sweet, and put up with my craziness so well! Thank you for joining me on this journey and being phenomenal cheerleaders and prayer warriors for these stories.

Beth Erin, you are an awesome beta reader! So willing and positive... and honest. Thank you for always being available and wiling to join me in my story-worlds.

Carrie Booth Schmidt, I am always in awe of you. Your big heart and love for books shines in how you inspire others. Thank you for being my friend and my co-journeyer.

Thank you, *Rachel Dixon*, for organizing my writing world. I'd love to place a clone of you in my personal life too – imagine how productive I'd be!! Thank you for all you do for me!

As ever, I want to thank *my wonderful family*, who encouraging me by talking with me about my imaginary friends and allowing me the joy of creating fictional worlds while living in a pretty remarkable nonfiction world with them.

And to the God who loves us just as we are but doesn't leave us there – instead pushes us to become all he's created us to be for his glory.

ABOUT THE AUTHOR

Pepper Basham is an award-winning author who writes romance peppered with grace and humor. She currently resides in the lovely mountains of Asheville, NC where she is the mom of 5 great kids, speech-pathologist to about fifty more, lover of chocolate, jazz, and Jesus. Her Mitchell's Crossroads series is a reader-favorite and her Penned in Time series has garnered national recognition. Her novels *Just the Way You Are* and *The Thorn Healer* released with a 4 1/2 star review from RT and a Top Picks rating. You can learn more about her books at wwwpepperdbasham.com and touch base with her on Facebook, Twitter, or Instagram.

ALSO BY PEPPER D BASHAM

Historical Romance
The Penned in Time Series
The Thorn Bearer
The Thorn Keeper
The Thorn Healer

Historical Romance Novella
Façade

Contemporary Romance
The Mitchell's Crossroads Series
A Twist of Faith
Charming the Troublemaker

A Pleasant Gap Romance
Just the Way You Are

Contemporary Romance Novella
Second Impressions

www.ingramcontent.com/pod-product-compliance
Lightning Source LLC
LaVergne TN
LVHW092205281025
824461LV00028B/191